BASED ON

the

GOOD DON

RICHARD MANCUSO
JACQUELYN GUTC

outskirts
press

Dedicated to those who sacrificed their own dreams so they could provide for their families during the Great Depression.

"Happiness lies not in the mere possession of money; it lies in the joy of achievement, in the thrill of creative effort."

— *Franklin D. Roosevelt, March 4, 1933*

Table of Contents

Foreword

I t's hard to use only a few hundred words to talk about my cousin, Sal. He was more like a brother to me than a cousin. And to my family, he was a caring person who protected us, whether we felt like we needed it or not.

Sal's role as protector in our family began at a young age. My dad was often out of town for work, and my mother was afraid of her own shadow, so when Sal was barely eight years old, he would come over and keep her company. Even though Sal was a kid, and one would think he could barely defend himself, his presence comforted my mom and made her less fearful.

As our family grew, so did Sal's vigilance over us. A great example of this — and one of my favorite Sal stories — was when my brothers and I made our Confirmation. My parents couldn't afford new clothes, so Sal and his brother, Joe, took my brothers and me to shop for new suits. Sal was an extremely dapper man in his own right. His dress was always in the latest fashion, and he was one of the best dressed in the neighborhood, so it was especially fitting that he would be involved in making sure we didn't have to wear old clothes to our Confirmation. My dad was a proud man and was upset that Sal and Joe had to buy the clothes for us because he couldn't, but it was such a kind and generous gesture that anytime I think about it, it makes me teary eyed.

When my brothers and I were a little older, Sal would sometimes let us help at the newspaper stand where he worked, so we would have spending money of our own. This kind of thing is a big deal to most kids, but was especially helpful and meaningful, because we were in the midst of the Great Depression. The fact that Sal could afford to give us work and money of any amount at a time when it was near impossible for adults to get work was yet another thing that made Sal stand out.

In addition, Sal supervised what we were doing, who we could pal out with, where we could hang out, and he did everything in his power to make sure that we spent a lot of hours burning off a healthy energy via basketball, boxing and gymnastics at the Riis House.

Thanks greatly to the close relationship Sal, his parents and siblings helped establish with my family more than a century ago, my family and the Mancusos continue to have the highest respect for one another and remain close, despite my immediate family moving to Alaska and the Mancusos mostly staying in New York.

The Occipintis are forever grateful to Sal for his love and generosity, and our lives were enriched by having him in our family.

C.J. Occhipinti (Connie)
Former Superior Court Judge of Alaska

Chapter 1
Hero of My Life

"We need to talk."

That was what my dad said when I picked up the phone on a sunny August morning. I had been relaxing, enjoying a cup of coffee and wasn't sure what to make of the urgent demand coming from the other end of the line in Upstate New York.

"OK, so let's talk," I replied.

"No, no ... we need to talk in person."

"Dad, what's so important that I need to get on a plane to hear it?" I questioned as I set my coffee down on the kitchen table, slightly annoyed that he was holding back.

"Just get out here," he urged. "We need to talk."

Unfortunately, you can't make a guy talk if he doesn't want to and when he is sitting on the other end of a phone line, seven states and 1,800 miles away. So about a week later, I found myself on an airplane traveling across the country on a four-hour flight from Denver to Newark. Although it wasn't quite that simple. I flew into Newark instead of Albany to save a few hundred dollars that I admittedly ended up spending anyway on a rental car, gas and tolls to get to my dad. Eventually, I learned my lesson and started flying straight to Albany, borrowing my sister's car when I got there. But this is a relatively recent development. That August, I was still going about it the old, stubborn way.

So that gave me several hours of travel time, including over 200 miles of solo drive time, to contemplate what could be so important that I was spending hundreds of dollars to speak to my dad in person. I just kept wondering what was going on. "Why couldn't he tell me over the phone?" I wondered. "Why do I have to make this trip? This is stupid."

After about four hours on the road, I pulled up to my cousins' house on Lake George where my dad was staying. Confused, tired, and frustrated, I chastised my dad in my head so much — continuing to have thoughts like, "This is ridiculous. What the hell is going on?" — that I hardly paid attention to the simple beauty of the house and the grand beauty of the lake whose front it called home and all of my memories of it.

Lake George was our summer hangout growing up — the South Shore, or Lake George Village, to be specific. My parents would take my sister Pat and me up there with several other families. Sometimes it was my dad's brothers and their kids. Sometimes it was his friend, Rip, and Rip's family. We kids couldn't wait to commandeer our own section of the beautiful beach. We'd spend the days taking paddle boats on cruises around the lake and swimming like fish around a roped off area designated for such fun.

Lake George felt like it was a million miles away from the inner city where we lived, and it might as well have been.

After all, it was worlds away. No horns honking on congested city streets or people yelling out in annoyance. No smog from smoke stacks, no rats scurrying from one shadow to another, no cold, mammoth high-rises cutting off the sun, no stench of the rotting garbage sitting out in front of the tenements. At Lake George, the cars would roll through the town, driven by people taking a break from boating who were running up to the store for barbecue supplies. The annoyed yelling was replaced by children laughingly calling to one another as we ran around playing in the hot, sparkling summer sun. And the smells were those of wild flowers and other beautiful fragrances of summer in the country.

Those summers at Lake George nearly ended when I was ten and we moved to Staten Island, having a new freedom to go out on our own boat at Mansion Marina, just three miles from our house. Midland and South beaches were just over a mile away, and I could see the ocean from my bedroom window. We loved to fish off the jetty, ride our bikes to the ocean, and play in the marsh. We always got to be out on some little adventure, and it felt like we lived the life of Huck Finn.

For a time, I visited Lake George more frequently when my sister Pat and her husband, Mike, moved to Albany when I was in my twenties. I'd visit the lake house with her family, eventually bringing my wife Carol and our two children, Chris and David, because I wanted them to be a part of those memories that meant so much to me.

But that was a long time ago, and when I rolled up the driveway, I hadn't been at the lake house in more than twenty years. A quick visual sweep of the outside told me nothing had really changed though.

This wasn't where Dad lived. He was the resident of a small, one-bedroom apartment in downtown Albany. But for this occasion, he'd asked the cousins if we could borrow their house. They'd agreed without hesitation. They didn't spend much time there anyway, since they actually lived sixty miles away in Albany. This just further confused me and piqued my interest. Whatever Dad wanted to say was so important that he needed to orchestrate an idyllic setting for the conversation to happen.

My white rented Ford compact crunched the granite rock of the short driveway. Driving only white cars was a habit I'd developed over my decades of life in Colorado, where the sun beats down so intensely that it makes any other color turn a car into an oven-like torture chamber.

As I slowly pulled in, I surveyed my surroundings, immediately noticing Dad's Oldsmobile parked in front of where mine would be momentarily. I took a deep breath, as I parked the car and got out, going around to the trunk to grab my suitcase. I wondered if I was really ready for whatever conversation lay ahead. Was it good news? Bad news? A family secret? Who else was in on this?

I pushed the trunk lid down and looked up at the house as I approached. There was no garage and it looked like a one-story from the front. Its looks were deceiving though, because the house was built on a hill and had two stories on the lake side, where there was also a boat dock.

The house was aging, but not obviously. Its light brown wood siding was in good shape and the house had been well taken care of by my mom's cousins.

I walked up to the front door, realizing that my dad must have been there alone, because there were no other cars around, and this wasn't the type of bustling urban area where people didn't need cars to get around.

I knocked on the wooden frame of the front screen door. Almost immediately, he appeared in my line of sight, emerging from the strong shadows of the late summer day. I couldn't imagine an instance where the smile on his face could be outdone by the huge one spread across it at the sight of me in that moment.

I opened the door, and it was easy to forget my concerns and frustrations over his demand that we talk face-to-face as a sense of calm and relief washed over me when my dad reached out to hug me. The door was barely open when I set down my suitcase and found myself in an embrace with the hero of my life. We kissed each other on the cheek as we had always done.

But it didn't take long after our embrace was broken before I was reminded why I was standing in the doorway of a house in Upstate New York with him. We'd hardly gotten through the "how was your trip?" small talk before he got to the point of my visit.

"We need to have a long, long talk," he said. "You know how I always called myself Honest Sal? I want you to know I wasn't always honest Sal."

Chapter 2
Honesty

Dad was eighty-seven years young at the time. It had been about a year since I'd seen him. Over the years, he'd made trips to Colorado to see me, or I'd headed east to see him. At that point, Dad had been on his own for a lot of years, having lost my mom to cancer thirty-three years earlier.

A former boxer, he kept a rigid exercise routine that people a quarter of his age would be lucky to keep up with. He worked out five days a week at the gym, jumping rope, swimming thirty laps in the pool, pounding a speed bag for twenty minutes, lifting free weights, and wrapping it all up with time in the steam room. Around this time, he'd told me he was cutting back on his exercise routine — maybe he'd cut back on the jump roping, he mused.

Dad was a specimen — a picture of perfect health, even shortly before his death at age ninety-three. Even in my forties with him in his eighties, I wouldn't have wanted to go head-to-head with him. But by the time of my visit that late August, his mind was starting to go. My family and I would see little signs that concerned us, mostly absentmindedness, like losing his car keys or forgetting to turn off the stove.

So I wasn't sure how concerned I needed to be about whatever he was bursting to tell me or how much of it was fact. He took it all very seriously from the beginning though and couldn't wait to jump right in.

When he gave me the line about not always being Honest Sal, I was a little curious. All my life, my dad had repeated the refrain, "You've gotta be honest." He was very tight-lipped though, so his sudden interest in talking had me surprised.

I said, "Dad, what do you want to talk about?" as he stirred in the kitchen, making cups of coffee for us.

"I want you to know I had my hands in certain things," he said. I became mesmerized by a golden sunset that would not be ignored dipping over the lake, with a reflection that created a painting-worthy image. Different from the stunning mountain views in Colorado, I thought.

My attention snapped back to my dad as I realized he was anxious to get talking, despite the evening hour.

"Explain to me why I'm here," I challenged him. "Couldn't we talk about this on the phone?"

"This needs to be face-to-face because I want you to know I wasn't always Honest Sal," he began to explain again.

Aware of the advanced time, I wasn't sure I had the energy to get into this conversation that night after all. The lack of energy reminded me of the overpriced airport food from what felt like a lifetime ago, and the convenience store snacks and copious amounts of Coca-Cola that sustained me all day.

I told my dad I needed food, and we headed to a Chinese

place nearby. It was one of the few restaurants dad could tolerate. He hated Mexican and refused to eat Italian out because nobody made it as good as Mom. So our dining excursions usually led us to a steakhouse or Chinese restaurant.

After dinner, I was refueled, but the full travel day had taken its toll. When we returned to the lake house, dad was surprisingly still eager to get to talking, but I was just too wiped out. I basically interrupted him to say that I had to go to bed and we'd catch up in the morning.

As I lay in bed that night, I thought of the only information I'd really gotten from him so far. "I want you to know I wasn't always Honest Sal," echoed in my head. I wondered what that could possibly mean, and it was the last thing on my mind before I slipped out of consciousness.

———— ⊕ ————

I slept in the next morning, finally rising around nine-thirty. I got much more than my usual nine hours of sleep, thanks to jet lag.

"I've been waiting all morning for you to wake up," Dad said when I walked into the kitchen.

The kitchen wouldn't have won a spread in "Better Homes and Gardens," but it worked. It was nice, clean and simple. It had the standard dark wood kitchen table, matching cabinets and Formica countertops.

"You want a cup of coffee?"

I said coffee sounded good.

I wasn't like Dad in most ways. Just one of them was that

he could operate on five hours of sleep a night but took two, half-hour-long power naps every day, usually around noon and four-thirty. With those little catnaps, he'd be ready to go at full steam again. I, however, need my nine hours. I remember how, all through my childhood, my sister and I would come home from wherever we had been and ask where Dad was, to which Mom would always reply, "The baby's sleeping." And sure enough, there he'd be — fast asleep on his back, arms bent and folded over his chest like he was in a casket.

Dad was also more serious about breakfast than I was. He was all about Cheerios or Corn Flakes with bananas and strawberries, or big breakfasts — the bacon and eggs kind of breakfast. He'd eat any or all of that along with endless glasses of milk. He went with the cereal option that morning at my cousins' lake house hours before I'd gotten up. I opted to skip breakfast altogether, except for the coffee.

I took my coffee out onto the deck and gazed across the lake, the late summer humidity not yet enveloping my lungs. Feeling refreshed after getting my required nine hours of sleep, I was ready to delve into whatever was on his mind.

"What the hell did you mean yesterday with the Honest Sal stuff?" I turned and asked as I heard him slide the door to the giant wraparound deck open and then close it behind him.

He settled into an Adirondack chair against the house that faced the lake. He held a fresh cup of coffee in his hand.

"That's what I wanted to talk to you about," he said, looking at me with an intensity in his eyes.

Everything about my dad was serious. Always. He was

what you'd call a man's man. Mostly muscle, he remained an imposing figure even in his advanced age, posting measurements of five feet, eight inches and two hundred pounds on that frame that boasted a wide chest. His hands were three times the size of mine, or at least that's how it seemed, even now. That intensity in his eyes now wasn't new to me — if he looked at you a certain way, you knew to freeze in your tracks. It was a linebacker stare that would put the fear of God into you.

He glanced down at his coffee cup, taking a sip.

"Back in those days you had to do what you had to do to survive," he began, looking back up at me. "Your generation, you've had it made all your life."

Chapter 3
Peter & Josephine

My father was born Rosario Peter Mancuso, in his family's apartment in Manhattan, on October 12, 1914. From the day he was born, Rosario was known as Sal, and legal documents were the only places where his birth name could be found. Sal was the fourth of seven children born to Peter and Josephine.

Back in those days, midwives were the norm, and they went to patients' homes to deliver babies. My father and his three older siblings — Tony, Joe and Murphy — along with his younger sister, Rose, were all born in the apartment on Henry Street. Phil and Connie were born in hospitals.

My dad was extremely fortunate to have the father he did. He would describe my grandfather to me as a husband and father more typical of today's society. I suppose what he meant by that was that his father was affectionate and loving and playful in a time when most fathers were not. Back then, the role of the father was to earn an income for the family to live off of, not be a playmate with his children. It wasn't unusual for men to work twelve to fifteen hours a day six days a week back in the 1920s. That's just how life was and what it was about. The mother was responsible for life at home — she was the glue that kept the family together. Wives and mothers were typically at home cooking, cleaning, and disciplining children.

The story was a little different for my father and his parents though. My grandfather was gentle and close to his children. He loved coming home from work and crawling around on the floor with the kids, wrestling and playing with them.

My grandmother, on the other hand, was a completely different story. Josephine Gallina was a baroness and very well-educated. Her life resembled romance stories that people tell of the rich girl falling in love with a peasant. This was despite the fact that her family's history was less than savory.

Josephine's father was from Rome. He was married, but was also a cheat and slept with any good looking woman he could. Eventually, the women's husbands started coming after him, and it was time to get out of town. He asked his father for the inheritance owed to him and settled in a small village in the mountains of Sicily called Resuttano. It was there where he laid eyes on Josephine's mother, the most beautiful woman he had ever seen. Although her father opposed it, you can't fight love, as they say, and Josephine's parents were married in Sicily, despite his having another wife with a family in Rome.

My grandma was the oldest child of their union, and she eventually earned what would be the equivalent of an associate's degree in business administration today. So her family was less than thrilled when she fell in love with Peter

Mancuso, the peasant. My grandfather.

Nevertheless, Josephine paid Peter's way to America. In 1902, she sent him to the U.S. to get established and call for her when the time was right. In 1904, she joined him in New York, where they married.

It would be hard to imagine coming across a more difficult woman than Josephine. She took crap from nobody, and I truly believe that my grandfather was the only man who could live with her. Grandma was stern — to put it mildly. She was cold and standoffish, and she gave the external impression that she resented how close my grandpa was to their kids. We had a joke in the family that if grandma were a man, she'd be "the head of the mafia."

Although Peter was a warm and loving father at home, he was no less serious or committed to working than any other man in the neighborhood at the time. Peter was a construction superintendent building skyscrapers that reached the clouds in New York City. This was an era when your job prospects could openly be helped or hindered by your nationality, and my grandfather landed many of his jobs because of his Italian connections.

Peter spoke fluent Italian and English and even knew some Yiddish. The latter he picked up from the neighborhood. I always say the neighborhood on Henry Street was like the United Nations. Other areas of New York City at the time were specific to certain ethnicities, but not ours. Our little neighborhood was home to mostly Sicilian people, but also Poles, Irish, Chinese, Spaniards, and Jews, and more. It was an incredible way to live and grow up to be immersed in such a variety of cultures, with people picking up different languages without really trying.

My grandfather, Peter, was the sole breadwinner, as was far more common in those days than it is today. So when the Depression hit and the stock market crashed, it was understandably devastating that Peter's job was lost, along with at least 13 million others. One-quarter of Americans lost their jobs during the Great Depression, and another fifty percent were forced to work for half their pay during that period.

My grandpa lost his job almost immediately when the Depression hit. All construction stopped in its tracks.

This Depression was something America had never seen before. Until 1929, there had only been panics, the violent stage of financial fluctuations like bank failures, market crashes, and even the anticipation of crises. The Great Depression was different, but the general public didn't know it yet.

Though out of work, families like my dad's got by on credit that landlords and shopkeepers extended to trusted customers in hopes that the financial troubles would be over soon and they would be repaid. Dad's family struggled through by these means for six months before he decided he needed to act.

I always knew my dad to be quick to help people in need, and this was no different. Though he loved learning and had plans of becoming an engineer someday, he decided to sacrifice his education for his family. So with reluctance, my grandparents agreed to let Dad drop out of school at the end of the academic year and become a newsboy. It wasn't easy — they knew he would probably never go back to school — but no one saw a way around it.

My dad was without a doubt the brightest, most intelligent person I've ever known. He deeply valued education, though he never graduated from high school or attended college, because life got in the way. I have no doubt that under different circumstances, he would have been an engineer. His parents knew how deeply he wanted to achieve that career, too, yet they couldn't forbid his quitting school to help the family survive.

Dad was a good student and a natural leader, so I wasn't all that surprised to learn decades later that he had been student body president and class president when he was in school. An interest in politics and education does seem to run in the family, after all. And it had always been clear to me that he valued academics very much.

From the time I was just a couple of feet tall, my dad would take me by the hand and walk me to the library around the corner from Henry Street on East Broadway, where he'd check out four or five books per week and devour them, reading them all cover to cover. He was self-taught, even learning algebra and geometry on his own.

It was like all that stuff — the dreams, goals, and desire to be in a classroom — was put in a box, and he had to close it up and move on, doing whatever was necessary to survive.

My father was fifteen years old when he dropped out of school in 1930.

His oldest sibling, Tony, was twenty years old and worked at the massive Fulton Fish Market, the most vital fish market on the East Coast since it opened in 1822, near the Brooklyn Bridge, above Fulton Street in lower Manhattan. Wholesale customers were the main buyers at the market, which still operates, in a new location in the Bronx. In 1924, 384 million pounds of fish were sold through the market, 25 percent of all seafood sold in the U.S.

Uncle Tony wanted to be a New York City cop, but couldn't apply until he was twenty-one, so he bided his time working at his future father-in-law's concession at the market.

Meanwhile, the second and third oldest children — Joe and Murphy — along with Rose, remained in high school. Phil and Connie were the youngest and stayed put in elementary school.

Even from an early age, my dad never acted without a plan. I remember how he had zero tolerance for talkers — he liked doers. He didn't want to hear what you were planning and would do someday; he would be impressed when you took the bull by the horns and made something happen. So it was with a plan that he quit school, not leaving until he secured a spot at a newspaper stand near City Hall.

Dad dropped out of school along with one of his closest friends, Johnny Kelly. They took jobs at the same stand working for two middle-aged Jewish brothers. The brothers would work Sundays, while my dad and Johnny rotated weekly twelve-hour day and night shifts.

1932

Sal Mancuso stuffed his huge hands into the pockets of his jacket as he stood in the shadow of the Third Avenue El train that rumbled past overhead. He had just started his fourth, twelve-hour shift at the newspaper stand that week. This week, he was on days. Johnny Kelly had nights.

The newsstand was about ten feet long and three feet wide with shelves going down the front to the ground, each holding the latest magazines. The top and front of the stand were filled with the day's evening editions of papers like the *New York Post*, the *Daily News*, the *New York Daily Mirror* and the *New York Times*, along with the smaller papers like *El Progresso*, the Italian paper. There were so many papers and magazines to choose from, but after working at the stand for almost two years, Sal knew the regulars and which paper they wanted every day, regardless of the headlines.

A guy who Sal knew worked at City Hall nearby greeted him with a quick "Afternoon'" as he picked up the *Mirror* and handed Sal two cents. As the pennies dropped into Sal's apron, he looked up to see the man walking toward City Hall with his newspaper already opened to the back, checking the previous day's racetrack results.

Time and again, the same situation would repeat itself. Every day, two cents would be handed over for a newspaper that would almost immediately be opened to the track results. It was kind of crazy that journalists worried so much about flashy headlines when people would really probably prefer race results to be on the front page, Sal thought, shaking his head as he watched the City Hall worker.

Chapter 4
Going into Business

It was a chilly fall evening. The air was brisk and New Yorkers were grateful for a reprieve from unusually warm September days that year. Sal approached the newsstand, ready to relieve Johnny for the night shift, though he was there a little early. He had something he wanted to run by his buddy.

"Hey," Sal said, nodding at Johnny.

"You're here kinda early aren't you?" Johnny asked. Sal was nothing if not punctual, but who wanted to be at their job longer than a twelve-hour shift required?

Sal had his hands in his pockets, looking down at the ground, kicking a cigarette butt away from the stand.

"Yeah ... I've been doin' some thinking," he said.

"About?" Johnny dropped two coins into his apron, nodding a silent but understood "thanks" gesture to the man who picked up his usual Mirror.

Lifting his cap from his head and running his hand through his hair, Sal started, "Well, you know as good as I do that practically every single person who buys a paper from us is barely walking away before they're looking at the race results, right?"

"No doubt."

"So what if we make it easy for 'em to pick a horse? What if we give 'em a way to make smart bets? We'll do all the research and improve their odds of winning."

"I'm listening …"

"Race sheets!" Sal said, his eyes bulging slightly with excitement. He looked around, realizing his eagerness may have gotten the better of him. In a more hushed tone, he continued. "I already talked to my cousin who takes printing classes in school. He thinks he can get the sheets printed without anybody knowing anything."

"And we sell 'em here?"

"And we sell 'em here," Sal confirmed. "And if we have to, we give the Wolzers a cut, but it'll be fine because everything we make will be clear profit. We can split it fifty-fifty. We could double the money we make just working here."

The seventeen-year-old boys saw dollar signs flash before their eyes. Just the prospect of doubling their income made the twelve-hour shifts at the newsstand more bearable.

Satisfied that his plan was in motion, Sal realized that he hadn't eaten anything all day.

"You want anything from Max's?" he asked Johnny.

"Yeah. You gonna keep me company and eat here with me so I'm at least not so bored for a little bit tonight?"

Sal chuckled. "Sure thing. The usual?"

"The usual," Johnny nodded.

Sal turned and walked over to Max's Busy Bee, the twenty-four-hour diner right in front of the paper stand on Ann Street.

Max's was a favorite of Johnny and Sal's. Max Garfunkel and his son Louis treated them like family. Max came to New York from Moldova in 1888 and opened his first Busy Bee on Ann Street, which was ultimately a failure and lost Max all of his money. But Max persevered and opened a second location down the street in 1896. That one was a success. It led to Max eventually opening fifteen Busy Bees around the city, and they became local legends known for serving everyone from business men to poor children. Max had a reputation for never turning anyone away and he and Louis took care of Johnny and Sal whenever they were at the newspaper stand. Plenty of times, Max or Louis would walk food out to Sal or Johnny without them even asking for it.

Walking up to the counter, Sal was greeted by Louis. They made small talk before Sal asked for two turkey sandwiches and two chocolate malts. He sat at the counter and pulled out a couple bucks while Louis got to work on the sandwiches. When he turned around and saw the cash in Sal's hand, he rolled his eyes.

"Put that away," Louis said. "How many times we gotta tell you, your money's no good here?"

"C'mon, Louis. Everybody's gotta get paid," Sal replied with a sigh.

"Yeah, and enough people pay us. You guys are good kids standing out there all day and night, and you gotta deal with the drunks stumbling outta here at all hours of the night. Just take the free food."

With a slight smile and look of exasperation, Sal folded his cash back up and put it in his pocket. Louis was right about one thing: Sal and Johnny certainly did deal with more than their fair share of drunks. People would stumble out of Max's, thinking they could get away with anything now that alcohol was legal again, or they'd be drinking away sorrows over a girl, and they'd tumble out of Max's and right into Johnny and Sal. The drunks seemed to feel inconvenienced by the boys' mere presence, most of the time, and were looking for a fight.

One fight in particular got out of hand and stood out above the rest. Sal was working the night shift when two Irish brothers were kicked out of Max's for trying to start a fight. They landed within just a few feet of newspaper stand.

Already agitated from whatever had prompted their desire to fight at Max's, compounded by their being thrown out, the Dillon brothers had no tolerance for the unamused teenager standing at the newspaper stand.

"Let's kill this Jew bastard," one growled to the other, judging Sal solely on his thick, dark hair and other stereotypes found in his appearance. The other guy showed his compliance by lurching toward Sal.

New York City wasn't an ideal place for a kid to work at night, even in the early 1930s. So Sal and Johnny kept a steel pipe behind the stand for encounters exactly like this one. Before either brother could get his hands on Sal, Sal brandished the pipe and began beating the two young men — who were five or six years older than he — without hesitation.

In what felt like an instant, the two men were lying on the ground, seriously beaten.

Looking over them, Sal's adrenaline rush that had kicked in when he went into fight or flight mode was suddenly gone, and he panicked, worried about the damage he had done to the wannabe wise guys. Sal took off running the more than half a mile home to go tell his brother Tony, the beat cop, who was off that night.

By the time they returned, a large crowd of both employees and customers had come out of Max's. It was a mix of people who wanted to see what happened and others who came to the aid of the bullies.

"Shit, Sal," Tony breathed as he approached the fallen bullies. A couple of guys gathered to help drag the Dillon brothers inside to resuscitate them. "Well, we can't say they didn't have it coming," one almost chuckled, lifting up one brother under his arms, from behind his shoulders.

As the two men got medical attention, Tony arrested them for assault. When their court day came, it was a sight to see. Sal, dressed in a nice, fancy suit with not a hair out of place, stood before the judge alleging that he had been assaulted by the bruised and bandaged men who sat in wheelchairs. Seeing the ridiculousness of the spectacle, the judge threw out the case.

That wasn't the end of it though. For the next six months, the oldest Dillon brother, Elmer, lurked around the newspaper stand at night, eager to pay back whoever had beaten his younger brothers within an inch of their lives. Elmer was in his early thirties, and rumor had it that he was the best pickpocket around, making enough money from unwitting New Year's Eve revelers in Times Square, that he wouldn't have to work for the rest of the year. Another legend had it that, while he was an altar boy, he once stole a priest's wallet as the priest stood at his altar in church.

It's hard to argue that the rumors weren't true. By all accounts, Elmer created quite the checkered history for himself. By 1936, he would be arrested forty-six times with twenty-two convictions against him with the New York Post writing how he had once been a "highly prosperous young pickpocket" around Chinatown and the Bowery. Elmer started getting into trouble with the police when he was a young kid of about nine years old and was recognized for his shoulder-length blond curls, which earned him the nick-name "Angel Face."

After a few months of regularly hanging around the newspaper stand, Sal and the Elmer became friends, and Sal felt compelled to fess up to the beating. He told his side of the story that had led to the brothers' concussions, bruises and broken bones.

Elmer knew his brothers well enough to know that Sal was telling the truth. He couldn't even be mad at Sal. Instead, he suggested that they go see his brothers when Sal got off work and this time, Sal was witness to a beating of the brothers by their older brother, who, ironically, didn't condone bullying and violence. He was, after all, just a pickpocket and an "Angel Face."

Chapter 5
Up & Running

Within weeks, Sal and Johnny had their race sheet business up and running, with the help of the New York City Public Schools, whose ink and paper were used without its knowledge.

The boys spent their slower night shifts researching the races and could hardly keep enough sheets stocked during the day. Their research allowed them to better predict which horses would win, place, and show, based on past races, and it was all outlined in the race sheets. The Jewish brothers who owned the newsstand allowed the boys to sell the sheets and didn't ask for anything in return. In fact, they admired the boys' entrepreneurial spirit. Really, no one put up much of a fuss. Selling race sheets was illegal, but not the kind of illegal activity that anybody really cared about. Cops who came by the stand looked the other way because in those days, people were struggling to make it and no one was getting hurt from this race sheet business.

Horse racing was unbelievably popular at this time in the New York area — not like today when most people only care about the Triple Crown races. Day after day, the tracks were nearly, or completely full. The country may have been in the midst of the worst economic meltdown it had ever seen, and the unemployment rate may have been upward of twenty percent, but that didn't mean people didn't bet. In fact, it seemed like everyone was placing bets — trying their luck with anything that could improve their financial standing. Never mind that the odds were against them. If a guy couldn't make it to the track himself, he had a bookie that could place the bet for him.

The race sheets were sold for five cents apiece. At that price and the quick rate at which the race sheets were being sold, Sal and Johnny's income skyrocketed as they made five dollars a day each in addition to the one dollar they earned from the newsstand. It was clear profit. Clear profit in terms of money, at least. Sal and Johnny put in countless hours of research every day and night, meticulously tracking each horse's races in the Greater New York area and its results in the newspapers.

This was the golden age of newspaper and there were dozens of newspapers sold in the New York metro area. That meant there were a lot of delivery people working and a lot of other newsstands in the city. And what that all meant was opportunity for Sal and Johnny. Before long, delivery guys saw what these teenagers had going on with the race sheets and wanted in. They offered to take the sheets to their other stops throughout New York City and Brooklyn for a small cut of the profits. The newspaper boys at the other stands would get a cut too.

Suddenly, Sal and Johnny were having ten thousand

sheets printed every week and their race sheets were making it all over the city to about a hundred newsstands. The only expense was their few bucks thrown to the delivery guys.

Things changed fast for Sal and Johnny. They went from being high school dropouts struggling to support their families, to entrepreneurs bringing in $250 a week, when the average man was making $300 in a whole year.

They didn't know what to do with their newfound wealth. When Sal would take breaks from his race sheet research, he'd be plotting how he could take his family's comfort to the next level. Thanks to Sal's ingenuity, Christmas had been brighter for the Mancusos in 1932 than it had been in a couple years. The children all had presents to open on Christmas morning and the family feasted on a savory roast. The younger children believed that Santa had found them once again, and Peter and Josephine were somberly grateful to Sal. Now, it was early spring 1933, and the wheels were turning about what more Sal could do for his family. He saw his breath as he stood at the newspaper stand, and it made him wish summer would come sooner. That's when it dawned on him that he had the perfect next gesture to help his family get back to where they had been.

Sal raced home after work, excited to share the news with his parents.

"Momma, Papa," he said, "we're staying at the beach this summer."

"Oh Sally, we'll be OK staying here this summer," Peter said, shaking his head. Josephine stood quietly, drying a plate with a towel, looking back and forth between her son and husband. It was a rare time when she didn't speak, unsure of what was unfolding.

"No, Papa, I know that you miss that summer escape we had for all those years until you lost your job. Summers out of the city, in the fresh air and walks on the beach. I can give that back to you. To us. To the whole family. And I'm going to. You'll never miss a summer in the beach house for the rest of your life. I'll make sure of it," Sal ended triumphantly.

Josephine stopped her drying as her lips curled slightly into a smile that most people would hardly even recognize as being there, it was so tiny. But her eyes glittered with excitement and admiration for her boy. Peter stood two feet away from Sal with his hands on his hips as his eyes began to well up with tears.

Summers at the rented bungalow on South Beach had been Peter's escape for as long as Sal could remember. It was all marshland around the house and just a quarter-mile walk to the beach. It was Peter's freedom and reminded him of his homeland in a way that the concrete jungle of the Lower East Side never would, and it had been suffocating to him to be unable to afford the rental for the past three summers. Over his years of unemployment, Peter had learned to give up much of his pride in himself and instead hand it over to Sal, who had become the provider. This gesture from his generous son was the latest in a growing list that had him beaming with pride and gratitude.

Peter looked up at Sal, tears in the corners of his eyes, and wrapped his son in an embrace. Sal took it in, thinking of how much he loved this man who was so kind and so openly appreciative for everything he did and gave. Every child deserved a Peter Mancuso in their life.

The Lake House

Dad told his story with ease. It was almost as if the 1930s were ten years ago instead of seventy. It was amazing hearing him take me back in time to the old neighborhood "between the two bridges." This was more than I'd heard my dad talk in my whole life. And yet, as he took a break in storytelling to go fix us a couple of sandwiches, I realized there was more. There had to be much more because he still hadn't shattered the image of "Honest Sal."

I always knew my dad dropped out of school during the Depression to work at the newsstand with Johnny Kelly. I never knew he had been so entrepreneurial at such a young age.

The noon glow of a fully exposed sun in the cloudless sky prompted us to eat our sandwiches inside. Dad devoured his and washed it down with a glass of milk, which was quickly covered in tiny droplets of condensation in the hot, humid air.

"So, obviously, I was paying off the bills and all of Mom and Dad's debts around the neighborhood," he said, leaning back in his chair.

I looked up at him as I chewed my sandwich, surprised that he just wanted to plow ahead in his story.

"The butcher, the baker, everyone was happy to see me when I walked into their shops," Dad said, leaning forward again and staring right into my eyes. "I was one of the only guys in the neighborhood who came in with cash in hand, every time." He pointed his index finger at me as he said it, helping to drive home his point.

"Things weren't getting any better for everyone else

though," he said. "For two years, I took care of my family and my aunt and uncle's. I still had extra money, but everybody else was still barely getting by. So," he shrugged, "I decided to start giving out loans."

Chapter 6
Keep Going

1934

On one square block in the Mancusos' New York City neighborhood, there were about twenty buildings on each side of the street, each one an average of six stories tall with four apartments per floor, totaling about nine hundred sixty apartments per block. With an average of ten people per apartment, that meant nine thousand six hundred people could live on one block. Just one block. And the Mancusos' neighborhood ran several blocks, from East Broadway to the East River and St. James Place to Market Street. That meant there were an awful lot of people in just one neighborhood struggling to come up with money to pay to live during the Depression era.

The Depression was many families doubling up in apartments to make living a little more affordable. It was seemingly endless lines of humiliation waiting for a turn at the soup kitchen. It was no meat and no ice to keep the icebox cold — which didn't matter much because there was often no food to put in it. It was no coal to keep warm. It was no gifts and no toys for the children. It was pure survival mode.

Sal wasn't the warm and fuzzy kind of guy, but saw an opportunity to help his family and friends and others in the neighborhood and jumped on it.

One afternoon, Sal sat in a barber's chair at his buddy Louie Amiano's shop, the wheels turning in his head. He had been planning this talk for days.

"Do you see a lot of guys in here needing money?" he asked Louie.

"Of course I do," Louie replied, not taking his eyes off Sal's jet-black hair as he worked fast with his scissors. "Everybody needs money these days. You know that. It's bad out there."

"Yeah, well, I think I can help 'em out," Sal said, staring back at himself and Louie in the mirror.

"Yeah? How's that?"

"Hey, let's just finish up here, then we'll go talk." Sal said it with a lowered voice as he glanced around. Suddenly his mind flashed back to two years before when he had the same experience telling Johnny about the race sheet idea.

Ten minutes later, Louie removed a white cotton cape from Sal's shoulders and Sal stepped down from the chair.

"I got a few minutes," Louie said, jerking his head toward a back room.

Sal followed him to a small, dimly lit room. He took a seat opposite Louie at a table littered with papers Sal assumed had to do with running the barbershop.

"So what's on your mind?" Louie asked.

"Well, you know, the race sheet business is doing good. Like, real good. So me and my family are all set. But there's all these other guys scraping to get by or getting turned down around the neighborhood because their credit's no good anymore. So I'm thinking I help 'em out and give 'em loans. Help 'em get through the week."

At this time, the banks weren't giving loans to people or small businesses, and the banking situation opened up a whole new opportunity for Sal.

Louie paused, staring at Sal. "OK ... so how do I play into this?"

"I want you and the barbershop to be the front. I'll give you a cut, but nobody can know this is my business — and I mean nobody." Sal looked Louie straight in the eye as he said that last part. It was the look that got more serious and fiercer the older he got. The look that told whoever was receiving it that Sal meant business.

Louie leaned back in his chair, looking up and making a steeple with his hands as he contemplated the offer on the table.

"Yeah, OK," he said, nodding. "I'm in!"

"Yeah?"

"Yeah," Louie smiled as he dropped his hands from the steeple and held one out to Sal. They shook hands, solidifying their new deal.

Sal had to swallow the excitement building in him as he walked out of the barbershop. He knew he was onto something big and potentially life changing for himself and those he was close to. The fact that his high interest loan business was a little bit of a risk — legally speaking — gave him a bit of a thrill too. He was starting to understand how guys in the neighborhood found the trajectory of their lives completely shifted with just a small taste of power and the money that could come with it.

With his fresh haircut, the hair on top slicked back, Sal crossed Catherine Street and rounded the corner to East Broadway as Patsy's bar came into view.

Angelo Fragapano, aka Rip, and Little Nick, both about six years older than Sal, were waiting in the dimly lit bar when Sal arrived at the time they previously agreed on. At nineteen, Sal was legally able to buy his own alcohol following Prohibition's official end the year prior. With purpose, he walked up to the bar where Rip and Little Nick sat, greeting them. The bartender, Gino Passarello, whose brother, Nunzio, owned the place, had already begun pouring Sal his beer when he saw him walking in.

Sal wasn't a big drinker and didn't generally approve of vices like being overindulgent in liquor or drugs, but he enjoyed a beer or a 7 and 7 and a cigar from time to time.

Sal cocked his head to gesture toward a booth, and Rip and Nick followed him to it, drinks in hand.

The three knew each other from the neighborhood and had been friends for all their lives. Rip was a lightweight boxer who hit like a heavyweight. At five feet four inches, he was a wiry but solid one hundred twenty-three pounds and fast. His nickname was rumored to come from one of two places: The first was the force behind his knockouts in the ring, which encouraged people to — what else? — rest in peace. The second theory was from an infamous card game that Rip was winning for a while, but lost in the end, supposedly making him so mad that he ripped the deck of cards in half. Either way, the stories made for the kind of legend you'd rather not mess with.

Little Nick worked as a laborer on the docks like most guys from the neighborhood did back then before the Depression. Nick was a six-foot, four-inch giant whose tree trunk-like legs matched the rest of his solid two hundred sixty-five pounds.

Sal idolized Little Nick and Rip for their strength and toughness, not to mention Rip's reputation in the boxing world. These guys knew the neighborhood, were intimidating, needed work, and Sal could trust them. They were exactly who he needed. It took no convincing on Sal's part to get them to agree to be the collectors in his new business venture. He knew it wouldn't. They would gladly get paid to go around intimidating people and picking up cash that people owed Sal.

"Try to keep the peace," Sal encouraged. "I'm not lookin' to whack anybody. Just make sure they would rather find a way to pay up than to see what happens if they don't."

The guys nodded and said they understood. Everything was set.

Chapter 7
Staying Invisible

Sal was discreet about his new business, careful not to ruffle any feathers. When he told Louie he wanted to be invisible, he meant it. Louie wanted the money bad enough and was eager enough to help Sal that he'd agreed. Sal was OK with that. Louie could handle himself. He wasn't so eager to get Johnny Kelly involved though. He'd told Johnny about his plan, but didn't let Johnny in on the action. It wasn't out of greed though; it was out of a need to protect Johnny. He couldn't let Johnny take the fall if things went sideways.

"Johnny, you're a good guy. I don't want to see you getting into trouble," he'd said, trying to let Johnny down gently. So they agreed that Johnny would take over the race sheets on his own while continuing to give Sal half the profit, and Sal handled the loan business solo.

Though he did his best to keep things quiet, Sal got a little help staying out of trouble. On one side was Alfred Embarrato, aka Al Walker. Al and Sal's mothers were cousins, and Al had a powerful position within the city: capo of the Bonanno crime family, one of the five major organized crime families in New York City at the time.

A capo, being like a lieutenant of a mob family, responsible for his own section of the family, is a hard-won position. Al Walker didn't get there by being nice. He lived in Knickerbocker Village between the two bridges on the Lower East Side of Manhattan and eventually became a powerful labor figure at the *New York Post*, where he was a plant foreman for three decades, though how much actual work he did there is questionable.

Though related, the Embarratos didn't have much in common with the Mancusos. The Embarrato family was mostly attracted to the wrong side of the law, while the Mancusos stayed straight. Mostly. And like most loosely connected families, the Embarratos and Mancusos only got together at weddings and funerals.

But that didn't mean that they didn't have each other's backs when it counted. Sal always believed that Al was partially responsible for the mafia leaving his loan business alone. The other half to the equation that helped Sal and Johnny operate under the radar was Sal's brother Tony. By 1930, Tony had made his way into the ranks of the NYPD as a beat cop, and like others in the neighborhood, he protected his own.

Back in the early twentieth century, at the peak of immigration to the U.S., the Irish had a leg up over the Italians and other ethnicities when it came to jobs because English was their first language. Of course the Irish brogue was thick, but that was still better than broken English, or none at all. That helped the Irish get jobs like cops instead of laborers, and it helps explain the Irish control of the NYPD at the time.

In the Mancusos' neighborhood in New York, Sal's family befriended an Irish beat cop named Tommy. Tommy had a heart for the immigrant and the Italian people. Unfortunately, the sergeant he was walking down the street with on a particular afternoon didn't.

One day in 1930, as Tommy and the sergeant — who left the priesthood in Ireland and became a cop in New York — walked the beat on Henry Street, they came upon Sal and Tony's mother, Josephine. The sergeant reached out and grabbed her arm.

"I hear yer son got in," he sneered at her. "They let wops in now. Guess they let anyone in."

Without a moment's hesitation, Josephine swung her purse and beat him over the head with it and he let go of her arm in shock, shielding himself with his arms.

Tommy stood to the side quietly chuckling and shaking his head.

"Arrest her!" the sergeant shouted at Tommy as he tried to move away from Josephine. "She's assaulting an officer!"

Tommy shrugged, a confused look on his face. "I didn't see anything," he said, winking at Josephine. Satisfied, she stormed off with her weapon calmly hooked over her arm.

Chapter 8
Heart of Gold

In the neighborhood between the two bridges, boxing was big in the 1930s. It was one of the few legitimate ways that guys saw to get out of the neighborhood and "make it." They'd start boxing, or they'd work at the docks, or they'd get into more illegal things. Sal was bound to get into boxing simply because so many people he surrounded himself with were.

Louie the barber wasn't always a barber. Before spending his days giving men a shave and haircut, Louie was a contender, even competing at the coveted Madison Square Garden.

Rip was a force to be reckoned with in the lightweight class. But his downfall came when he was pushed through the ranks too quickly and encouraged to fight middleweights who weighed thirty pounds more than he did. One jaw-busting shot ended Rip's boxing career after just two years and twelve bouts in the ring.

Influenced by his friends and the neighborhood, Sal began stepping into the ring as a middleweight when he was seventeen. He won every fight by knockout. His style was to wait for his opponent to drop his guard before attacking. Everyone in Sal's circle was excited about what he could accomplish and the level he could reach — everyone except his mother, that is. Proud that a long string of KO's were left in his wake, Sal wanted to go pro, but Josephine put an end to that. When she said there was no way in hell her son was going to be a boxer, Sal — as many good Italian sons do — listened. He did, after all, have other means to earn money and respect in the neighborhood.

———— ((●)) ————

Thanks to Sal, the Mancuso family was returning to financial stability. Sal's father, Peter, had helplessly watched four years go by without work and without being able to bring anything, literally or figuratively to the table. He gained weight and became frustrated, beating himself up over his lack of ability to provide for his family.

Sal knew it would help his father mentally and physically if he had a job to go to. A way to feel productive again. Sal wracked his brain over how to help, but obviously there weren't many jobs to be had and Peter was far from the only former breadwinner out of work. Eventually, Sal had the opportunity to make a job for Peter, just like he had made his own. He had been thinking long and hard about what kind of work Peter could do, when he walked by a storefront across the street from his family's apartment on Henry Street one day and noticed it was vacant. That's when the idea hit him.

A candy shop. Candy was easy to buy with little commitment and everybody liked it. The shop could sell other items that people would want every day, like newspapers, magazines, cigarettes and cigars. To top it all off, Peter could sell his homemade Italian ice, a neighborhood favorite. Upon deciding it was the ideal operation for his father, for reasons including its lack of physical demand, Sal got the shop up and running within a matter of weeks, not discussing it with anyone until he was in the throes of opening it. Sal hired Peter to manage the shop, which was nestled at the bottom of a six-story tenement building, four steps below street level. Its windows peeked out over the street, announcing its presence to the world with a red and white striped awning.

The store was no doubt heaven for the kids who stopped in, taking their pick between Wrigley's gum and a dizzying array of loose candy. What was really popular though were Peter's Italian ice treats. He had a special method of taking the slushy ice and water mix in and out of the freezer in thirty-minute intervals to help get its coveted fluffy look. The lemon flavor was by far the best seller — when people paid, that is — but Peter also whipped up strawberry, cherry, coffee, and pistachio flavored Italian ice too.

It was a great idea for everyone involved. Almost everyone, that is. Peter had a purpose again and Josephine happily got time away from him. But Sal didn't exactly make out from the deal as he intended.

Day after day, he'd ask his father how things were going. Peter would respond saying things like, "Today was a good day!" But Sal found that the cigar box where the money was kept was always short of what should be there for the amount of candy that was gone. He quickly realized what was going on and he was furious.

"Papa, are you giving candy away without people paying for it?" Sal asked.

"Ehhh, the kids wanted it and didn't have any money. You should've seen their faces!" Peter would say as his eyes lit up.

As good as Peter's heart was, his business savvy was not. He continued to run the business this way, mostly giving handouts to kids, and Sal continued to float it. It was simply a giveaway store, and every kid in the neighborhood knew it.

Sal didn't understand his father's way of thinking, his lack of business sense and what Sal considered the weakness of a kind heart. But while Sal may have looked down on that kind heart in the business world, he was not immune to softness himself — he just didn't see it that way.

As Sal continued to build his neighborhood empire, not only did he see people who were struggling enough that they'd jump at the chance to take out loans from him (or Louie, rather), but he saw over a dozen families that he felt compelled to help in any way he could, at no cost to them. And help them he did. The neighborhood looked after its own and Sal was part of the fabric of that neighborhood. During the worst days of the Depression, seventeen families plus his own had Sal to thank for keeping them afloat, the closest of which was his Uncle John and Aunt Angelina's family. While helping other families came as a result of new money from the loan business, Sal took on the responsibility of Uncle John's family shortly after the race sheet business took off. Angelina and John were like a second set of parents to him, and their kids were like his second set of siblings.

Despite his irritation over Peter's kindness, it was actually that kindness that brought Uncle John into the family in the first place. Sal was just a few years old when his father brought a stranger home — the stranger who moved in with them and would later marry into the family.

When Peter stopped in his usual Italian coffee shop in the neighborhood one day after work in 1912, he saw a man sitting at a table crying. The man was small in stature and had a thick, jet-black mustache that matched the hair on his head, which was parted on the left. Concerned over the unusual sight of a grown man crying in public, Peter asked the barista at the counter what was going on. The man explained that the guy who was crying had been swindled by his own brother. The brother had convinced the crying man to come to America from Italy. They started and ran a successful oil and wine importing business together, but the brother suddenly took all of their money and went back to the Old Country, leaving the man penniless with an inventory he was now in debt over and rent due for a storefront that he couldn't pay.

Peter hardly took time to process the story before he sat next to the crying man, John Occhipinti. He wanted to get more of John's story but more importantly, help him out. As they sipped on coffee, John told Peter his story, still seemingly in disbelief of it himself. There was something about the story he relayed and the way he did it that convinced Peter that John really did seem like a good, trustworthy guy, just down on his luck.

Peter suggested that John come home with him and stay

with the family that night. He'd help John get on his feet — and introduce him to his single sister-in-law, Angelina, who happened to live with them too.

Angelina arrived in the U.S. about five years after her sister, Josephine, Sal's mother, and moved into the Mancusos' apartment, where she had stayed for about three years by the time she met John. Peter's hunch to set the pair up and to trust John paid off. The couple were quickly smitten with one another. They both lived with the Mancusos, where Josephine kept a watchful eye on them for the first two years they dated, plus another seven that they were engaged. When they married on April 24, 1921, Sal was six years old.

Angelina and John rented their own apartment across the street from Sal's family, and as Sal grew up, he spent countless hours over at their place looking after Angelina when John was working. He would always remember spending so much time with her and running errands around the neighborhood for her — the most embarrassing of which was buying nylons. So it was without question that when Sal provided for his immediate family, he would also provide for his extended family, the Occhipintis. At the time that the Depression hit, John and Angelina had four children, and John lost the cabinetmaker job that Peter got for him during better times.

Helping his own family and Uncle John and Aunt Angelina's was just the beginning for Sal, and his new lending business made it possible for him to extend his reach.

Word travels fast in a neighborhood like the one between the two bridges, whether it's good news or bad, so Sal knew who needed help and who he could provide it to. When he decided that he was in the position to help a family close to him, he was generous and gave assistance with no strings attached. In no time, Sal was paying rent for seventeen families with the money he was making from the loan business and race sheets. Sal was making more money than he knew what to do with. He was also falling in love.

Joanna Farina, always known to friends and family as Jenny or Jean, had exotic looking green eyes and light brown hair with red highlights that looked copper when the sunlight caught her hair the right way. The best friend of Sal's younger sister Rose, Jenny was a soft-spoken junior in high school when she met Sal. Of course she had known who he was. They both grew up on Henry Street, after all, and everybody knew everybody in the neighborhood. But until the introduction from Rose in 1934, they didn't actually know each other.

Sal was two years older than Jenny and he impressed her. He wasn't like the boys in school. Sal was a man, with his own businesses and fancy, custom suits to fit the role. No matter where he went, Sal was the best-dressed guy in the room, wearing a suit and tie from Phil Kronfeld's and top-shelf leather shoes. He always had money on him, was self-confident, and was known everywhere he went. She was smitten.

It didn't take long after the couple began dating for her sweet demeanor and generous spirit to help put Sal's new-found fortune to good use. She inspired him to go beyond paying the basic bills for families in the neighborhood. Together, they would unload toys for children's birthdays and an abundance of gifts for Christmas from the trunk of

Sal's slightly used, but top-of-the-line, black 1934 Buick. Thanksgiving saw home deliveries of turkey dinners with all the fixings, and at Easter, there was ham. When a man longed to buy his wife something special for her birthday or an anniversary, Sal and Jenny were there to help him out. But none of the generosity bestowed on the couple's friends was done with any fanfare. Careful to never embarrass the parents or the man of the house, donations of any kind were always given quietly, discretely, in cash when money was involved, and out of range of the children. When kids woke up on Christmas morning, they knew nothing of the no-strings-attached kindness and generosity of Sal and Jenny. They simply knew that their parents had come through and that was all that mattered to everyone.

Chapter 9
Giving & Sharing

The Lake House

Dad gazed past me as he talked about the gifts and money he and my mom brought to all those families. It was as if he was transported back to that time as he talked about how grateful people were to have not just one thing, but several things for their kids to open on Christmas morning. He talked about how he and my mother would make their way up multiple flights of stairs in tenement buildings, arms overflowing with awkward-sized boxes and bags.

"Your mother absolutely loved going and picking out gifts for the kids," he said, a small smile peeking out from his lips as he stayed inside the memory for a moment longer. "She wanted to buy all the toys in the whole freakin' store. I'd have to remind her that we had a lot of other kids to buy for too. But it was great. She always knew just what the kids wanted. I had no idea." He shrugged.

"We'd go home feeling so good about ourselves," he said, looking back at me. "Sometimes, guys would cry. That was hard to see. I'd stick a $10 bill into a guy's shirt pocket, right after he told me it was just so hard and he was worried about how he was gonna feed his kids, and he'd tear up, thanking me. They'd always try to be tough, but times were just so hard. Guys were worn down. I'd just put a hand on the guy's shoulder and tell him it was no big thing, just something to help him until he got back on his feet. But sometimes it was like that ten was the motivation he needed to keep going, keep trying, not give up. That ten let him walk into the meat market with his head up high, knowing he didn't have to try to make a deal with the butcher."

There was a pause in his speaking, and I took in the weight of his words, the weight of his actions and what he'd done for all those people.

"So it was kind of like you were a modern day Robin Hood, huh?" I asked, grinning a little.

Dad raised his eyebrows, making a face as he considered my simplified definition.

"I guess you could say it was something like that."

I thought about my mother, my sweet mother, going along with my dad's actions. He did these amazing things for his friends and neighbors, but he was loan sharking to do it. Taking advantage of other people's unfortunate situations to help others out of theirs.

"Did mom know about all this? Where the money came from? Was she OK with it?" I asked.

"She knew but she didn't know. She didn't flat out ask and I didn't flat out say. But there was enough talk and she was a smart woman. It wasn't even that bad, though," he said. "We weren't operating like Capone and those guys. Nobody was getting hurt. If Little Nick or Rip came knocking at your door, you'd find a way to pay, too," he said chuckling. "There were threats a few times, I guess, but mostly what we were doing was more like offering payday loans and you know that racket is legal now!"

I couldn't argue with that. Dad and Louie were giving out weeklong loans at 20-percent interest. They'd get one dollar back for every five dollars they loaned out. These days, payday loan places can charge an annual interest in the triple digits. At least people weren't in debt for the rest of their lives after taking out a loan through my dad and Louie — they had no choice but to repay within a week. Their business worked out for everyone. The borrowers got to stave off eviction or hunger and dad treated his friends and family to a lifestyle they could only have dreamed of a couple years before.

Chapter 10
True Love

1936

After two years of dating, Sal and Jenny married on January 2, 1936. Sal was twenty-two, and Jenny was twenty. They were a perfect yin and yang match and the loves of each other's lives. She was calm, quiet with a gentle hand, while Sal was a hit first, ask questions later kind of guy.

The wedding ceremony was in the neighborhood at St. Joseph's Parish with the so-called atheist Sal biting his tongue. The Catholic wedding took place during a time when hours of pre-marriage classes weren't required and even someone like Sal who was strongly atheist, or agnostic on a good day, could be married there, by a priest he could not stand.

The ceremony was followed by a typical style wedding for the neighborhood, what's known to Italians as a "football wedding." Family and friends gathered at the Riis House, an institution for gatherings in the neighborhood, and stuffed themselves with cold cut sandwiches on Italian bread, even tossing sandwiches to each other through the air, like footballs.

The happy couple took a honeymoon to Niagara Falls, where Sal contemplated his new life as a married man, with responsibilities to his new bride. For weeks leading up to the wedding, he debated whether to leave his job at the newsstand and get a "real" job — an adult job. Through his financial rise, Sal had kept the newsboy job for legitimacy. He always thought the mobsters who were just known mobsters were ridiculous and stupid. Without a front or a day job, he'd say, "How do they justify not working, but driving a Cadillac, wearing expensive custom suits and monogrammed shirts?" So no matter how much of a moneymaker his illegal businesses were, he'd never give up work that he could show on a tax return. Johnny continued to work at the newspaper stand and run the race sheet business, of which Sal continued to get half of the earnings.

Sal decided to give up his job at the newspaper stand and took a position as superintendent of the Riis House. The place where their football wedding reception was held, the Riis House was like an earlier version of a YMCA, where kids from the neighborhood could play sports, work out and learn boxing. Sal and Jenny moved into a beautiful apartment in the Riis House that came with Sal's job. Housed on the top floor of the three-story building, the two-bedroom apartment faced Henry Street and had all of the best amenities for the time. They had the perfect situation that allowed Jenny to be a homemaker and Sal's goodwill ambassador around the neighborhood.

The Riis House was at 48 Henry Street and was a pillar of the neighborhood. Formerly the King's Daughter's

Settlement, run by the Episcopal Church, it relocated to Henry Street from a temporary space in 1892. In 1901, the building was renamed the Jacob A. Riis Neighborhood Settlement House in honor of the man who advocated for the poor and helped secure both temporary and permanent residences for them.

Riis was from Denmark and went from being a poor immigrant to a social reformer, publishing a then unparalleled exposé on the deplorable conditions in the slums on New York's Lower East Side called *How the Other Half Lives: Studies Among the Tenements of New York*. The Riis House offered sewing classes, health care, summer camps, and eventually opened a gym in 1906, for which Riis was congratulated in a letter from Theodore Roosevelt. Riis died in 1914, at the age of sixty-five, but a friendship with Sal's father helped forge a long relationship between the Mancusos and the Riis House.

The whole family spent countless hours there participating in boxing and gymnastics. Sal's brother, Joe, eventually became the athletic director, helping Sal land the superintendent job. He was hired by the executive director, Helene Nelson, who knew the family well and paid Sal a nice salary that complemented his other activities. As facilities superintendent, Sal was in charge of making sure the building was clean and in the best condition. He also taught boxing there, which was a major benefit for Sal, who loved the sport long after his days as a fighter had ended.

Chapter 11
Friendships

Sal's loan business was doing so well, he had more money than he knew what to do with, and his legitimate job and living situation helped ensure that he had nothing to worry about. He'd work all day at the Riis House overseeing repairs and maintenance, and cleaning and buffing floors, then come home and take one of his catnaps, recharging before going out. Late in the evening, Sal would change into one of his fine custom suits to get ready for a night out with his boys.

By the time the loan business was in full swing in 1936, Sal had an impressive entourage of guys who went everywhere with him. The thing about an entourage is that it makes anybody look like somebody. A guy could walk alone down the street and no one would pay attention. But put him in a circle of five, ten or fifteen guys, and people will take notice and wonder why he's so special.

Sal's entourage was made up of guys from the neighborhood, most of whom he'd known his whole life, and most of whom were down and out during the Depression. Most of their families were part of the group he financially supported.

He trusted them and they trusted him. And the perks they got from hanging out with Sal weren't too bad.

If their wives had qualms with the late night carousing, it didn't seem to matter. Twice a week, Sal would round up his buddies and take them on New York adventures only celebrities and mobsters of the time could relate to. If there were rock stars in the 1930s, they would have shared a lot of the same experiences as Sal and his Bowery Boys.

Sal's guys weren't exactly the storied Bowery Boys that spawned hundreds of books and movies. But they were, in a way, filling those big, legendary shoes of the nineteenth century gang with their own incarnation. They were, afterall, walking the same streets in the Five Points neighborhood.

The Bowery Boys of the mid-1800s was a nativist gang that was anti-Catholic and anti-Irish. Members were on the more youthful side of life and were known for being criminals who employed violence and had an anarchic spirit, yet they typically held legitimate jobs as printers, mechanics and other tradesmen. The Bowery Boys would participate in bloody turf wars with rival gangs of the area, but were politically minded. In fact, many of their fights were with people who supported the opposition to whomever the Bowery Boys had thrown their support behind for political office. The gang created its own slang and wore fashion that separated members from others in the Five Points area. The Bowery Boys had their heyday around the time of the Civil War and eventually broke into several factions, ceasing to exist by the nineteenth century.

Since then, many other young gangsters would be associated with the Bowery, including Lucky Luciano, Al Capone,

Meyer Lansky, and Louis "Lepke" Buchalter. But while they all participated in illegal activities, Sal Mancuso and his gang refused to go as far as their many predecessors often did — they never murdered anyone.

Sal's crew was made up of tough but good guys. It included guys with names like Sonny Scarletto, Frankie Shoes, Blackie Saraceno, The Preacher, Ceci, Louie The Barber, Milty Feldman, and of course, Johnny Kelly, Rip and Little Nick.

They spent nights out carousing in the city, but loved weekend escapes at the beach. Sal and his gang reveled in getting away from the city grime to go tuna fishing in Sheepshead Bay in Brooklyn, using a boat bought in Little Nick's name called the "La 4 Tuna." They'd sit in the sun all day on the lookout for schools of blue fin tuna that would run through in August and early September. The boat was their man cave of sorts, an escape where they could horse around and be away from every worry.

"La 4 Tuna" was an all-guys hangout, but on many of the warm days when the sun would cause the water to glimmer, Sal and his buddies would pay five cents and take their girls on the ferryboat over to South Beach or go to Coney Island — the epicenter of summer fun in New York.

Like a habit that was somehow always exciting to give in to, the guys met at Patsy's bar for a few drinks to start off their night, every time. Then, they'd walk across the street to Chinatown, which, at the time was a mere four blocks long — a fraction of today's Chinatown that spans five times that area. They'd fill up on chow mein and chop suey on Sal's dime, as with the drinks at Patsy's, before piling in to three or four spacious DeSoto Skyliner cabs that would carry them north to Midtown. Destination: Madison Square Garden.

At the time, Madison Square Garden was the mecca of professional boxing matches in the New York area, with fights there a couple nights a week. Lesser-known pros, along with the biggest boxers of the day, fought there weekly.

Even back then, it was no small — or cheap — feat to gain ringside seats, but Sal did it. Whenever he and his gang would show up for a fight, they'd be ringside, right up in the action, cheering or booing for the powerhouse man of the moment.

The Lake House

"I felt like a king back in those days," Dad said.

By now, the sun was getting low over the lake. I looked at my watch, not believing how many hours had gone by as I sat enthralled with my dad's time travel back to the Depression. He had barely taken a break after lunch and continued to tell his stories throughout the rest of the afternoon. I never knew he was capable of speaking so many words in a month, let alone one sitting.

I suggested we grill a couple of steaks Dad had in the freezer and take advantage of the nice weather. It was late enough that the temperature had cooled as the scorching sun lowered, but the humidity still hung thick in the air. It hit me like a weight as I walked onto the deck with the steaks on a vintage white Corelle plate in hand, outlined with that classic green floral pattern that screamed 1960s.

Right behind me, Dad seemed unfazed by the sudden cloak of humidity pressing down on us. He was a native New

Yorker, after all — one who hadn't ever left. It occurred to me that I'd gotten too used to that dry western heat of Colorado, but I wasn't exactly sad about it. New York had never really felt like home to me anyway.

"You know I knew Tyson?" he asked, lumbering up beside me as plumes of smoke rose up from the grill.

"Huh?"

"Tyson, Mike Tyson. I told you I knew him, right? It was crazy all the people I met from the Riis House and going to the fights at the Garden."

He had told me. I had always been impressed with all the people my dad knew and maybe even more importantly, who knew him. For a small family in a little patch of New York, it was amazing how connected the Mancusos were to so many famous — and infamous — people.

Long past fighting age, Dad still coached boxing and was always passionate about it. Somewhere along the way, he met Cus D'Amato, the famed manager and trainer of Mike Tyson, Floyd Patterson, and José Torres who all ended up in the International Boxing Hall of Fame. Cus moved to the Catskills after Patterson and Torres' careers ended, and my dad would spend weekends there, where Cus had opened a gym. Cus took in Tyson and adopted him when he was a teenager. I remember my dad relaying that Cus was excited because "he got a heavyweight champion again." Cus died in 1985, just before Tyson earned that title.

It's fair to say that over his long career, Cus D'Amato had what my dad could have had — if he'd wanted it. As the 1950s wound down, Dad was approached by Angelo Dundee about a partnership that would have had him grooming kids to prepare them for professional boxing before passing them off to Angelo. Dad turned down the offer though, skeptical of the business. He'd already seen too much corruption behind the scenes, like coaches arranging for a fighter to take a dive.

Dad was also a top pick to be a coach of the 1960 U.S. Boxing Team. It was another opportunity he dismissed.

He had come to think of boxing as a way for kids in the neighborhood to learn to defend themselves and burn off their energy without getting into trouble. The gym gave them a sanctuary where they could gain confidence and feel good about themselves. Professional boxing was entirely different and Dad didn't want any part of it.

As my dad stayed between the Two Bridges coaching neighborhood kids, the 1960 Summer Olympics in Rome helped establish the great Muhammad Ali as he took home a gold medal. When Ali returned, Angelo Dundee coached him for the rest of his time in the ring and would go on to train fourteen more world champions, including Sugar Ray Leonard and George Foreman over a legendary, six-decade career.

Chapter 12
Generosity

1937

S al had no shortage of friends, and he gained more respect by the day, thanks to his generous giving. This was despite that fact that he scorned religion while being surrounded by deeply Catholic family and friends.

His mistrust in the Catholic Church began at a young age, thanks to one particularly harsh, greedy priest, Father Vincent Januzzi. The priest locked horns with Sal's mother because she disagreed with his demand that parishioners pay twenty-five cents per family member who attended church, including children who would sit on their parents' laps.

When Sal made his Confirmation, Father Januzzi required $10 from each godparent. Sal's godfather put in $5, and Sal was sent back by the priest to tell his godfather that Father Januzzi said it wasn't enough. So his godfather put in $1, and Sal was confirmed.

Sal would later brush off Bible stories he read to his children, assuring them that the stories were simply fiction, but they set principles by which people should live.

But Sal's desire to help when needed was stronger than his anti-religion sentiment. Friends and family lined up to name him their children's godfather. In all, Sal became the godfather of more than thirty children from between the bridges. On one particularly fateful day, Sal sat wearing what to other, churchgoing people would have been their Sunday best, but for him was a normal day's suit, as dozens of kids — including one of his godsons — waited to be confirmed. The old priest who made Sal feel bitter toward the church so many years earlier announced before the congregation that a dozen children wouldn't be getting confirmed because their godparents couldn't pay the fee. Refusing to stay seated while innocent children were humiliated in front of their family and friends, Sal stood and said he would be the godparent to each of them too. He paid the $10 per child for his godson and the twelve other kids who needed help.

Just as he discreetly supported families in the neighborhood, Sal quietly donated to the church, for reasons no one would really ever know. When Sal wanted to give to the Church, he did so through Mazie Phillips, "Queen of the Bowery." Mazie was part owner of the Venice Theater on Park Row and beloved in the Bowery for her generosity and kindness to the area's derelicts, eventually rising to legend status beyond her little portion of New York. A platinum blonde with a husky voice whose throne was, by all accounts, the ticket booth at the theater, she befriended Sal when he was a little kid. Mazie was about eighteen years older than Sal and had always had a big sister kind of role in his life.

Mazie was one of the few people from the neighborhood who didn't have any need for financial help from Sal or anyone else. Their friendship had no strings attached and existed because they genuinely liked each other. She was a larger than life entrepreneur who was beloved for her big personality and generosity. Mazie supported herself and philanthropic efforts through her half ownership of the single-screen, 600-seat theater and bumper cars and other concessions on Coney Island.

Although she was Jewish, Mazie was known to donate to three Catholic churches in the area: St. James, Transfiguration, and St. Joseph. She was rumored to have been so involved in the Catholic Church that she even went to confession. Although it may have seemed odd to some that a Jewish woman would donate money to Catholic churches, she clearly didn't care. This made her an ideal person for Sal to funnel money for the church through, and that's what he did. Although Mazie donated her own money, Sal also discreetly gave her his own cash to give to St. Joseph's and other places that would help those in the neighborhood — wherever she saw fit. He trusted her.

Sal found no shortage of ways he could help the community he cared so much about. From surprising, discreet church donations to Christmas parties at the Riis House complete with Santa Claus, to paying rent for those he was close to, Sal loved finding ways to help those in need. Some activities, like the church donations, were more discreet than others, but no matter what, he took care of his own. For some, like his family and the members of his gang, the benefit of being in Sal's inner circle spanned far beyond free drinks, Chinese food and boxing matches.

As passionate as he was about education, Sal never sought

THE GOOD DON

a formal education again after dropping out of high school. By the time he was making good money, he had a wife, the financial responsibilities of dozens of people weighing on him, and soon after, a child on the way. But he always wanted other people to have a shot at an education that would mean making it beyond a day job at the docks or doing something illegal to make a living. It was in that vein that he paid for friends of his to attend college.

Juan Carlos Ortega — better known as J.C. in the neighborhood — and Sal were like brothers. The Spanish J.C. was an only child and moved across the bridge to Brooklyn with his mother — his father was a Merchant Marine and often gone — but still dated a girl from the old neighborhood. He didn't have any money, so Sal would give him what he needed to get back and forth for visits. In exchange, J.C. would hang out with Sal during the night shifts in his newspaper stand days to keep him entertained. Eventually, J.C. became one of the guys Sal helped get through college, paying for him to earn his bachelor's degree from the nearby Brooklyn College.

Sal couldn't have known then — and neither could J.C. — but that education would pay for itself hundreds of times over as the years went on. J.C. went on to take his college education far, becoming a vice president at one of the largest pharmaceutical companies in the world. Living the high life, J.C. eventually owned luxury homes in Mexico and Miami and spent decades making numerous offers to Sal to come work with him. Jenny never wanted to leave their home in New York though.

Sal was in his late fifties when he and J.C. were getting ready to retire. J.C. offered Sal a small ownership stake and a position as head of logistics in a new pharmaceutical company he was starting. He promised Sal and Jenny that they would live like royalty in Mexico, and to everyone's shock, Jenny agreed to go. Over the years, Sal had been offered positions around the world in Japan, Alaska, Spain, Germany, Italy, but turned them all down because Jenny didn't want to leave her aging parents. This time was different. J.C.'s charisma, charm, and salesmanship made the offer too enticing to turn down. But the whole deal came to a tragic end when J.C. suffered a massive coronary upon returning to Mexico. J.C.'s death brought the entire venture to an abrupt end, which meant Sal and Jenny would stay in New York.

Sal also loved buying fancy gifts for people. When Tony got married, Sal bought him a beautiful Chrysler. This was the way people elevated themselves in the neighborhood and showed their success — with nice, expensive things.

Chapter 13
A Deep Hurt

Summer 1937

The summer of 1937 brought irreversible changes for the Mancuso family.

After almost eight years of essentially being unemployed — only kept occupied by the candy store — Peter Mancuso was called back to work. But although he remained the same gentle soul he always had been, the near decade without real, paying work had taken a toll on him. Peter had gone from a strong one hundred fifty pounds on his five-foot-six-inch frame, to a round two hundred fifty pounds, and the years of not being able to provide for his family battered him mentally and emotionally. So when his former employer called him back to work on skyscrapers that were again seeing construction, Peter and his family had mixed feelings. Everyone was happy to see him return to work, and Peter was undoubtedly happy for the opportunity to be the breadwinner again, but his health was deteriorating, and the new job was as a laborer, not superintendent, which he had been before the Depression hit. It was hard to imagine a fifty-four-year-old man, weighing 250 pounds being a full-time laborer, but Peter didn't complain.

It was a longer haul to work than it would be on a typical day because the family — including Peter — was soaking up every last day of summer available at the rental house on Staten Island. He woke up on a Friday morning in late August to catch the train from South Beach to the ferry in St. George that would take him to Manhattan where he picked up the train.

He worked all day in the hot, late summer sun, wondering how he allowed himself to get so oversized and out of shape while being angry at the Depression that left it idle for all those years. He was tired, but he made it through the day, and that felt good.

Peter arrived home that evening to a bustling but relaxed beach house with Josephine busy at the stove, and the kids, Phil and Connie, lazily listening to the radio after a long day at the beach. They were all happy to see him, happy he'd gotten back on the job, but something didn't seem right. He seemed exhausted and his breathing seemed strained.

"How was it?" asked Josephine as Peter lumbered over to give her a kiss hello.

With the sun shining in the kitchen window, she could see sweat beading on his fair-colored forehead. That wasn't unusual, except that he seemed so tired and his breathing was louder and strained. Her eyes lingered on his face for longer than usual.

"Oh, well ..." Peter started, sighing and slightly rolling his eyes. "It was nothing like candy store work." He let out a brief chuckle before being overcome by a coughing fit.

"Peter, are you OK?" Josephine asked, her back to the stove now, as her eyes became glued to her husband. "Maybe the day was too hard on you?"

"No, no ... you worry too much," Peter assured her, pushing away her concerns with the dismissive wave of his hand.

She frowned. Josephine Mancuso was not easily blown off.

"You go lie down and rest," she demanded of him.

"I'm fiiiiine," Peter said as he shuffled back to the living room to play with the kids.

As the evening wore on, Peter slowed down even more as the tightness in his chest began to concern him more and pain he hadn't experienced before also settled in his chest. But not wanting to worry his family, he said nothing and pretended not to notice Josephine's hawk eyes on him all night.

But in the middle of the night with the sky still dark, the crickets chirping, and clammy breeze from the marsh flowing into the house, Peter awoke suddenly, too worried about the worsening pain to ignore it anymore.

"Josephine," he whispered, cringing in pain. "Josephine," he said again, this time a little louder and waking her.

The moment she opened her eyes to tense whispers of her name, she knew what was happening. It was what she had feared since her husband first walked through the door from his first day back at work that evening. She had felt somewhere inside her that all was not well with Peter. But she hadn't called the doctor because Peter was so dismissive of her concerns that she didn't know whether she could justify calling the family doctor in all the way from Manhattan.

"What is it? Are you in pain?" she asked the shadow of her husband as she bolted upright in bed upon hearing her name.

"Yes, yes," he replied, struggling to inhale. "I need to go to a hospital."

She could not make any more justifications or waste any more time, so she ran from the bedroom in a panic and rushed to the phone to call for an ambulance. She was particularly grateful to have the telephone in that moment because she knew that it was a novelty for many.

An ambulance arrived within minutes, announcing its arrival through a deafening siren that had the Mancusos' Staten Island neighbors sleepily staring out their windows, eager to see what the commotion was about.

As the children cried in alarm, ambulance attendants did a quick check on Peter before loading him into the ambulance. Josephine quickly changed into an outfit more acceptable for being seen in public than her nightgown and insisted she go along with her husband while a neighbor agreed to watch the children.

On the ride to the hospital, Josephine held Peter's hand while she explained to the ambulance attendant what she had witnessed in her husband's behavior after his first day back to work. She was calm and collected as she told the men that Peter just didn't seem himself and that his tiredness and strained breathing seemed to be more a bad sign of things to come than simply the result of a man's hard day at work. The attendants asked Peter questions, encouraging him to relay his version of the day's events and what got him to the point of being rushed to the hospital, but he was scarcely able to project more than a few words forming a broken sentence at any one time, and Josephine urged him to rest.

As the day began to break, Peter was whisked away to a hospital room, after assuring Josephine that he would be OK and would see her soon. With a tear almost visible in her eyes, she somberly told him that she knew he was right.

With Peter being evaluated by doctors and the situation out of her hands, Josephine found a hospital payphone and put a call through to Sal.

Jenny heard the phone ring from its perch on a wooden table in the hallway. It was hardly dawn, but she was up early as always, enjoying the quiet time while Sal slept off a late night. She rushed over to pick up the receiver, eager to grab it quickly, before it woke Sal who had blown into the apartment just an hour or two before.

"Jenny," Josephine said upon hearing her daughter-in-law's sweet voice greeting her. "I need Sal. Get him up."

"Mom, what is this about? What's wrong? Sal is sleeping."

"Of course he's sleeping. That's why I said to get him up," Josephine snapped. "He needs to get here. To the hospital. His father needs him."

"I don't understand. What is going on? What happened to Pop?" Jenny asked, feeling a knot tie itself in the pit of her stomach.

Exasperated as if Jenny's inquiry was ridiculous, Josephine replied impatiently. "We don't know, Jenny. Maybe a heart attack. We just got to St. Vincent's. Tell Sal to get here immediately." And she hung up.

With tears flooding her eyes, Jenny tried to process the idea that her beloved father-in-law was in trouble and that there was apparently an urgency for those who wanted to see him to get to the hospital.

"Sal!" she yelled, too loud for the small apartment. "Sal! Wake up!" She rushed into their bedroom and over to the side of the bed that Sal was sleeping on. She gently shook him. "Sal. It's Papa. Wake up. He needs you."

Sal's eyes fluttered open, taking in the sight of his beautiful wife for a moment before his brain processed the tears running down her cheeks and the meaning of the words she was saying.

"Sweetheart, what is it?" he asked as he sat up and met her gaze.

"Your Papa. He's at St. Vincent's. Your mother said they think it's a heart attack, but they don't know. She says you need to get there right away."

Sal wasn't sure how to process what his wife had just told him. Sal wrapped his arms around Jenny as she sat on the bed and leaned into him. Something was wrong with his father. He had been able to fix everything else that had been a problem for the family, but now he was faced with the grim reality that he might not be able to fix this.

Within moments, Sal was dressed again and he and Jenny were en route across the bay to Staten Island where Peter lay in a hospital bed.

"Momma," Sal said as he walked briskly toward his mother and embraced her. "Where is he?"

She pointed to a room next to them. Sal grabbed Jenny's hand and wasted no time striding into his father's room.

Walking into the tiny hospital room and seeing his oversized father looking pale, in a hospital gown and lying there with his eyes closed and hooked up to an IV, Sal stopped just inside the door and finally understood what people meant when they figuratively said they felt like they'd been punched in the gut all while he tried to swallow a knot that he suddenly felt in his throat. He felt Jenny look at him as she squeezed his hand.

"You take a minute with him," she said to Sal, blinking back tears. She gently kissed Sal on the check and was gone. Then it was just Sal and his father. Peter's eyes fluttered open and a slight grin spread across his lips as he saw Sal standing there, looking dapper even in a time of crisis and holding his hat in his hands.

Sal took a spot in a chair beside the ugly, white, steel bed and reached for his father's hand.

"What's going on, Papa?"

"Oh Sal, they don't know. They say my heart isn't as strong as it used to be and it's giving me troubles."

"So what are they gonna do about it? You want me to talk to 'em? We'll make them help you however they can. Money doesn't matter," Sal said, a combination of anger and desperation in his voice.

"You're a good boy, you know that Sal?" Peter asked, ignoring Sal's questions. "You're a good boy and you take care of everyone and you don't even realize how generous you are." Sal didn't know what to say.

"You're a good boy and you've done more for the family than I ever could."

"Papa, I —"

"No, Sal, listen. When I couldn't provide for your mother and your brothers and sisters, you did. You were just a boy and you did more than I ever could. You need to think about how much the family needs you. Not just us but Jenny now too, and the family of your own that you might have someday. They all need you more than ever. I don't think I'm going to make it. I won't be here to help if something happens to you. It wasn't such a big deal before when I could help, but I'm going to be gone and it's going to be all up to you. You need to stay safe and cut out that nonsense."

"I don't know what you're talking about, Papa," Sal started, but Peter shook his head.

"Sal. I know I don't know everything you're into, but I'm smart enough to know that no one makes the kind of money you're bringing in doing honest things these days. You've always thought about your family, and that's why you were a good boy. But it's time to be a good man and think about your family in a different way. Instead of thinking about how you can spoil them, think about how you can stay safe to keep them safe. Use your head and be smart."

Sal took a deep breath as he let go of Peter's hand and sat up a little straighter. He felt like his father's weak eyes somehow had the strength to melt his big ego into a puddle.

"Promise me, Sal."

Sal took a long moment, looking away from his father and staring at a spot of nothing on the sterile looking white wall. He ran his fingers through his hair before settling with his head in his hands for a moment.

"I'm smart, Papa," he said as he looked back up into his father's face.

"I know," Peter said.

"And I don't mess up."

"Not yet."

Sal rolled his eyes. "Look, Papa, you've got nothing to worry about. I'm not going anywhere and I will always take care of the family — all of it. I'll stay safe. I've always stayed safe."

"All it takes is one mistake, Sal. One screw up. And if you go around thinking you're always the smartest guy in the room, you're never gonna see the smarter guy coming."

Sal couldn't believe his dad was even talking to him about this. Peter had never asked any questions, never tried to tell Sal how to run his life, and now he wondered if Peter had just been waiting for the right time, or if the threat of life cut short was getting to him.

"Papa, I always want to make you proud. I will always do my best to make you proud. I can promise you that."

Peter Mancuso died from a massive heart attack later that day — on Sunday, August 22, 1937. He was fifty-four years old.

The family was at a loss without Peter. Josephine had been the dominant one in the family, but Peter was the rudder that kept the family moving forward, on course. When no one could handle Josephine's harsh outbursts or biting words, Peter would sternly say, "Josephina! Basta!" in her direction, saying, "Enough!" and without another word, she would drop whatever had riled her up, letting the target of her words take refuge. In all, it was Peter's calm demeanor and gentle love and playfulness that kept the family going, even while Sal provided the financial support.

Sal recognized this as much, if not more than, anyone and was devastated over the loss of his father. They were such different people and didn't always understand each other, but they had a special relationship, and Sal had great reverence for his father. Memories of childhood laughter and rolling on the floor playing or practicing karate with Peter would flood Sal's mind at random times in the days and years following his father's death and with it, another piece of his childhood — what little remained since the Depression — fell away. He had received the last piece of parental advice he would ever get from his father. A desperate yet forceful plea to go straight and guarantee that he would stop doing anything that would possibly take him away from the family that needed him so much. As words that Peter chose to not speak until he was on his death bed, Sal knew that the plea held more weight than most attempts that parents made to control an adult child's life. The conversation with his father drifted around his brain day in and day out, but Sal wondered how he was supposed to walk away. What would he do? His father admitted that Sal provided for the family like no one else had or could, so how was he supposed to do that without the revenue streams that gave the family that financial support and security? He couldn't deal with that now. For now, the memory of Peter's watery, sad eyes and pleas to Sal would have to settle for rolling around in his mind and being pushed around by more pressing matters. For starters, there was saying official goodbyes to Peter.

Sal was, of course, prepared to pay for a final resting place for his father, but that turned out to be one concern that he didn't have to burden himself with. Peter's younger brother, Charlie, had died fifteen years earlier and was buried in Newark at one of three plots purchased by Charlie and his wife, Anna. When Peter passed way, Anna told Josephine and Sal that she wanted Peter to have her plot and be buried next to his brother. That settled it.

Despite his own beliefs, or lack thereof, Sal saw to it that Peter had a traditional Italian Catholic funeral service, and old Father Januzzi, of whom Sal remained deeply contemptuous, led it. Josephine and her youngest children filled the first pew. She sat stoically looking straight at the casket, while the children around her fussed, cried and were cared for by Aunt Angelina and Jenny who comforted them, putting their own sorrows aside.

Sal's gang all attended the service looking dapper, but never quite outdoing their leader. They somberly shook his hand at the entrance of the church, hugged him and expressed their condolences, each in his own way, before taking their seats. Sal sweat through his black suit, hating that the day had to be so damn uncomfortably hot, as if the events of the day didn't make it uncomfortable enough. He couldn't shake the feeling that the weight of the world on him was somehow getting heavier.

The timing of Peter's death had Josephine and the youngest kids, Phil and Connie, moving back to their Henry Street apartment days before Labor Day, only a few days earlier than usual. It was hard for Sal to go back to that apartment and see his newly widowed mother raising the kids on her own. The only bright spot he could see in the situation was that he and the other grown kids — Tony, Joe, Murphy and Rose — were close by and could support the family.

In the midst of the heartbreak Sal suffered over the loss of his dad, he remained particularly grateful for the opportunity to continue to support his family when they needed him, as they had for nearly a decade. And he was proud of his ability to give generously to friends and those in the neighborhood who needed help, regardless of what his dad thought. But the life that gave him those abilities to help others wasn't without some level of inherent danger, that was fair to note. After all, loan sharking was illegal and people weren't just sent a friendly bill when they owed money; Rip or Little Nick would come knocking and make a guy tremble in his shoes if he couldn't pay. Not to mention the fact that what Sal was doing was really mobster kind of stuff and he was lucky the wise guys didn't come knocking on his door, expecting him to bow out of the business. But Sal didn't feel too much worry for those reasons. It was his father's pleas weighing on him and eventually, his mother would turn up the heat on him, asking when he was going to go straight. She offered stern reminders that the family had already lost Peter and was relying on Sal more than ever. It was like she knew what Peter had said to Sal on his deathbed. But no matter what she said and no matter how moved Sal was with his father's last words to him, there was no walking away from the business. There was too much on the line now — his entire family's well-being.

Chapter 14
Feeling the Pressure

The next several months went by with the Mancusos in a haze of learning to move forward without their patriarch. So the family especially welcomed the joyous news that Jenny and Sal were expecting their first child. Even Josephine seemed to have a little more bounce in her step.

Patricia Mancuso was born on May 18, 1938, in Manhattan, and from the first moment he saw her, Sal was struck by a profound urge to protect this tiny person from any and all injustices and suffering in the world — at all costs. Suddenly, his own ego and the protection by his cop brother, Tony, and his relation to Al Walker didn't seem like enough. After all, if Sal was honest with himself, he would have to admit that he was always looking over his shoulder — watching for the police, but mostly other organizations and their made men. But this was something no one really knew about him. Being a man of so few words, Sal internalized his worries and carried on every day as if he was totally comfortable with the life he and his family were living. But with Patricia's birth altering his world and his inherent need to protect his family, Sal's perspective began to change as his worries slowly became too big to ignore.

And as if all of this wasn't enough, there was more pressure. Pressure from people who were even more powerful than Sal's parents and child — at least in terms of politics and the law.

Tony was no longer just a beat cop by 1938. He was fighting organized crime. In 1935, Governor Fiorello H. La Guardia named Thomas E. Dewey as special prosecutor to battle organized crime in New York County. Dewey received his own staff, offices and budget, and operated separately from the district attorney's office. Tony was one of about sixty cops who Dewey chose to be part of the task force.

In 1938, Dewey was elected as New York County district attorney and was well respected for his hard-hitting attitude on crime, a major departure from the previous eras of the district attorney's office. The legal community loved him for this and had come to know him well from his time as special prosecutor, when he earned a reputation as a "racket-buster" going after organized crime.

Some of Dewey's major initiatives during his early days as DA in 1938 were creating the Rackets Bureau and Frauds Bureau, and establishing a team of accountants who would investigate financial crimes. That year, Dewey picked a dozen men from the NYPD to be part of the organized crime task force and tapped Tony as the lead detective, heading it all up. Over the years, Tony would become Dewey's right-hand man, both figuratively and more literally as he was always seen at Dewey's side.

Tom Dewey and Tony Mancuso's friendship meant

Dewey was a frequent dinner guest at Josephine's apartment, often visiting weekly for years. This was how Sal got to know him. Even though Sal did his best to keep his business quiet, Dewey was quick and smart, had his ear to the ground, and had enough sense to know what Sal was into. Dewey was always friendly to Sal, and vice versa. But he hated organized crime, and it was part of his job to wipe it out.

But rather than putting loud, vocal pressure on Sal to get out of the business, he was more subtle about it, making comments here and there about Sal's "work" and how "the business" was going. Dewey mostly kept quiet about it — especially in front of Sal's family. But there were a few occasions over the years when the two men would find themselves in close proximity to one another without anyone else around. One hot summer night in 1938 brought about one of these instances.

When dinner at Josephine's apartment ended, Sal excused himself, slipping out and downstairs where he could sit on the stoop for a few minutes, getting some fresh air as the sun sank below the buildings around him. Or at least the air was fresh in the sense that it was somewhat cooler than the stuffy, stifling air trapped inside his mother's second story apartment.

Sal had barely sat down when he heard the door open behind him, and looked up to see Dewey walking toward him.

"Leaving so soon?" Sal asked the district attorney.

"You know, the work's never done," Dewey replied, stopping to stand beside where Sal sat on the steps. Sal stared straight ahead, his arms extended out over his knees, with his hands clasped together. Dewey looked down at him.

"Hey Sal, you've really gotta think about what you're doing here."

Sal's jaw clenched a little, but he didn't give any other signal of having heard Dewey.

"Seriously, Sal. You know I care about you and your family, and if my guys don't get wise to what you're doing, there are other, scarier guys, who will, if you get my drift. You've got a little baby in there now. You've got a legitimate job. You don't need to be running whatever you are out here on the streets."

After a beat, Sal looked up at Dewey's face with its dark mustache, filling in all of the space between his nose and upper lip.

"Thanks for the talk, Tom," Sal said in a clipped voice.

"C'mon, Sal."

"I got it. Thanks, Tom. Have a good night."

Dewey let out a deep sigh as he looked out across the street in the fading light.

"OK, Sal. You too. Just think about what I said," and he made his way down the steps, the jacket of his cement-colored, pinstriped, three-piece suit slung over his arm in the sweltering heat.

—◁((◉))▷—

Despite the mounting pressure to get out of loan sharking and his increasing stress over it, Sal was still able to find joy in the generosity that the business allowed him to have.

He paid for parties at the Riis House in the fall that featured pumpkin carving and apple bobbing, then Christmas parties with Santa in December that children and their families were always excited to attend. The parties gave them all a break from worrying about their lack of a job or inability to pay for the next meal.

Sal made sure that activities at the Riis House were inclusive at a time when that wasn't so common. Every person who came through the door of the gym was given the opportunity to shine in an activity. For the kids, there was gymnastics, baseball, boxing, and track and field. There was dancing and social nights for adults and special basketball games organized for paraplegic men, most of whom were left that way from the war.

There were always events happening at the Riis House, but Sal's main passion was coaching kids in boxing. Kids as young as seven years old would come for training several times a week. He put together an impressive program that taught the kids self-defense and discipline, and gave them an outlet for their angst and energy. These kids didn't have to worry about defending themselves in a neighborhood fight when they had training from Sal.

Sal's students got the opportunity to compete, thanks to his efforts to bring in boxers from other clubs for matches. On his own watch, Sal organized the competitions and out of his own pocket, he paid for the ribbons and trophies the boxers won.

The boxing program introduced Sal to more people around the neighborhood who would become legendary in their own right, including Henry Modell and his son,

William, who ran Modell's Sporting Goods on Cortlandt Street in Lower Manhattan — the predecessor to what would become a one hundred-fifty-store chain spanning the Northeast. Modell supplied Sal with all of the ribbons, trophies, boxing gloves, and other sports equipment he needed to run the Riis' activities.

But particularly important to Sal was his relationships with the kids. They were incredibly appreciative to him for all that he gave them, and they admired him.

The Lake House

I had to laugh a little thinking about my dad teaching boxing at the Riis House. Even years later, long after we'd left the old neighborhood, my dad continued to coach at the Riis houses in Harlem and Bedford-Stuyvesant, believing in the value of self-defense and the self-confidence he was helping kids gain.

"I remember walking out of the Riis house with you and all the kids just hanging on you, wanting to protect you and walk us all the way to the El train," I said to my dad, smiling thinking about how much everyone had always loved him. But I noticed the look on dad's face was changing. It wasn't surprising that he wasn't smiling with me. A cousin once asked my Uncle Murphy if dad ever smiled and his answer was that, yeah, he did. Before the Depression. But in this moment with him, he was almost frowning, deep in thought.

"Dad, are you OK?" I asked, focusing on the eyes that weren't even noticing my presence.

Breaking out of his thoughts, he said, "I think that's

enough for today. I'm tired." He grasped the wooden handle on the side of the recliner he'd told his stories from over the evening, and with a pop sort of sound, folded in the footrest part so he was sitting upright. I was caught off guard by this abrupt ending to our day, but we had turned on the lamps a couple hours before as the sky became dark, so it was pretty late and he had had a long day of drudging up memories from half a century earlier. He was probably just feeling emotional after reliving his dad's passing, I figured. And Dad wasn't one to show that he was feeling emotional, so I left it alone and didn't ask another question as he said goodnight and shuffled off down the hall to his bedroom.

The next morning, I slept a little later, still not used to the time difference and was lulled to stay in bed by the steady rain beating on my bedroom window. But then I remembered the reason for my visit and decided a dreary day was better than most for story telling.

I showered and dressed before walking into the living room to see my dad had taken up residence in his recliner, engrossed in the newspaper.

"Mornin', Dad."

"Hey, Son," Dad said, looking up over his reading glasses at me. "Get yourself some breakfast."

"You need anything?"

"Nah, I'm good, I'm good."

I poured myself a cup of coffee, struggling to even consider breakfast, as usual.

I walked back into the living room where my dad sat and struck up a few, non-Depression-era-related conversations with him, and he was back to being the tight-lipped man I'd always known before the previous day. But he had sucked me in. My brain was still stuck in the grimy Lower East Side from years before my birth, where Dad had left it the night before. I didn't want his stories to stop. I didn't want that drawbridge to go back up, bringing him back inside himself again.

"So, what stories ya got for me today?" I prodded. His nose was back in his newspaper.

"Huh? Oh, I don't know. Maybe later. I told you pretty much all of it," he said dismissively, not tearing his eyes off the black ink before them.

"Dad, I've only got one more day. If you've got stories to tell me — and I think, and hope you do — you've gotta tell me now," I said.

Silence.

"Dad, I —"

He held up a hand silencing me. "What do you want to know?" he asked.

I couldn't believe this. The guy couldn't stop talking — had to practically be forced to — for the last thirty-six hours, now he was acting like I was bothering him by being curious.

"Are you kidding me? You called me here. You wanted to talk. You couldn't stop talking for the last day and a half. And you're just done? I don't know what I want to know. How about how the story you're telling me about being a hot-shot neighborhood Robin Hood ends?"

He laid the paper down across his lap and folded his hands on it. When he looked up at me, I knew this was serious. Those eyes. You didn't want to mess with the man who those don't-fuck-with-me eyes belonged to. But there was more in them than hardness I was used to. I swear I saw a glint of a tear. I held his gaze steady with mine.

"You remember how I said that I laid down the law for Rip and Little Nick when we got started? I told 'em we weren't gonna be whacking nobody?" I nodded. "Well, unfortunately, there weren't a lot of other guys doing the kinda stuff we were doing who had that same kinda code."

Chapter 15
Another Blow

1938

Baby Patricia started wailing as the pounding on the door threatened to shatter it into pieces. Jenny rushed to the crib and swept the baby into her arms, shushing her gently as she started swaying side to side to calm the child. Sal shoved his right eye against the tiny peephole in the door and saw Rip's face magnified in it. He ripped the door open.

"Goddammit Rip!" he roared. "What the hell do you think you're doing? Are you stupid? You wanna wake up the whole friggin' neighborhood? Because you're off to a good start with my kid! I got a screaming baby to deal with now thanks to you. What are you doing here anyway? We aren't meeting the gang for another hour!" Sal stopped seeing red just long enough to notice the uneasy look on Rip's face. Rip never looked uneasy, and now he looked down at the ground.

"Rip," Sal said, more gently now. "What is it? Why are you here?"

"They found Johnny," he said, his voice cracking as he looked up to meet Sal's eyes. This wasn't good, Sal knew.

His eyes narrowed and his thick eyebrows furrowed. Johnny stopped showing up at the newspaper stand three days earlier and everyone was on edge looking for him and trying to find out who might know something.

"What do you mean they found Johnny? Who's they? Where?" Sal felt like his heart was pumping so hard and so loud that he was the one who was going to wake up the neighborhood.

"The cops. They found him in the East River," Rip said, his eyes tearing up slightly and his lips pursing immediately, as if he was afraid that more horrible news might escape from them if they weren't closed tightly. From inside the apartment, Patricia continued to wail.

Sal felt like he was the one in the water, drowning. He felt like he couldn't breathe and his legs couldn't hold him up anymore. He turned and leaned with his forearm against the doorway where he and Rip stood. His forehead fell into his arm and squeezed his eyes tightly. He shook his head against the wooden doorframe.

"No," he whispered. "No. Goddammit, no."

He stood like that for a few moments while Rip stood silent in the hallway, outside the apartment. He didn't know how to handle seeing Sal like this. He didn't know how Sal could take a blow like losing Johnny. Especially losing Johnny like this.

Sal inhaled deeply and lifted his head before punching the doorframe that had just held him up. "Those goddamn bastards," he hissed, the fire quickly returning to him, lit by immeasurable pain. He walked inside and sat on the sofa, leaning forward so his forearms draped over his knees. Rip followed him in and sat in a chair across from Sal.

"Who did it?" he asked Rip, looking up at him through red eyes.

Rip shook his head sadly. "They don't know. Word is they found him in the water off Pier 6. Looked like he'd been in there a few days."

At this last sentence, Sal dropped his head into his hands. Johnny. Poor, sweet Johnny. His best friend and partner in schemes big and small since they were just kids. His best friend and partner who he'd done everything to protect from the bigger crimes. His best friend killed and left floating in the filthy East River.

"They're damn cowardly sons of bitches," Rip said. "You know that. Don't have the decency to deal with things any way but whacking somebody. Johnny didn't even do nothing." Sal didn't look up. He ran his hands through his hair. His chest hurt. His stomach knotted. He felt tired. Too tired.

"He was associated with me," Sal whispered. "Does his mother know?"

"She just found out. Kept saying it couldn't be her Johnny. That it had to be a mistake." Silence. "We'll get 'em back for this, Sal. We aren't gonna stand for this. They can't just whack Johnny and think nothing's gonna happen to them."

"No," Sal said sternly. "I told you we weren't going there. I've gotta think about this."

"But, Sal —"

"Rip," Sal commanded, "you better go. And don't do anything stupid. Don't do anything I don't tell you to do. Just go home. Or go tell whoever else needs to know. But don't go after nobody. Just keep cool."

Wordlessly, Rip stood up.

"I'm sorry, Sal," he said, looking down at Sal.

"Me too, Rip. Me too."

After the door clicked shut behind Rip, Jenny emerged from the baby's room.

"Everything OK?" she asked. She had gotten the baby calmed down and back to sleep in her crib. Sal lifted his head from his hands and reached out a hand to her, pulling her toward him. "Johnny's gone," he said looking up into her eyes.

"I know. He's been gone for three days, Sal," she said standing in front of him, facing him. Looking up at her, Sal's eyes welled up with tears that flooded from his eyes and he lost control, grieving for his friend. His brother.

"Oh my God, Sal," Jenny breathed, kneeling in front of him. She took his face in her hands, one on either side. "Sal, he's …" But she didn't finish. Sal buried his face in her chest as he cried and she wrapped her arms around him, tears streaming down her own porcelain smooth face. "I did it," Sal cried into her charcoal gray nightgown, his body heaving as he cried harder. "I did this to him."

Chapter 16
A Little Crazy

The coroner's report said Johnny died of asphyxiation by submersion — he was drowned. And his body was believed to have been floating in the East River for three days before it was discovered by a young couple walking along the pier on July 30, 1938. Johnny's mother and her sister had gone to claim his body, and Sal had insisted on going with them.

If it was possible for Sal to speak any less than he already did, the days following Johnny's death where when he exemplified that. Jenny and Josephine were worried. So was the rest of Sal's gang. The difference between them was that, while Jenny and Josephine felt confusion and sorrow over Johnny's death and heartbreak for Sal, the gang wanted revenge.

It was dusk on the day of Johnny's funeral. The whole gang — Rip and Little Nick, Sonny Scarletto, Frankie Shoes, Blackie, The Preacher, Ceci, Louie the Barber, and Milty — gathered in the comfortable shadows of Patsy's Bar to raise a toast to their fallen brother. It had been a grueling day that found Sal inside the walls of St. Joseph's once again, feeling too broken to care much that it was the despised Father Januzzi leading the service that gave the final farewell to one of the most important people in Sal's life.

After the Mass, a small group of mourners, including Sal, Jenny, and the other guys, watched over Johnny's burial, but Sal had felt like he was in a daze the whole time, thinking maybe he finally knew what having an out of body experience felt like.

Once they were all congregated at Patsy's, Gino Passarello had shut the doors to outsiders, flipping a "Closed" sign toward the street.

"What gives?" Rip had asked.

With a shrug and the wave of a hand, Gino replied, "Forget about it. We don't need any wiseasses in here tonight. Tonight's just for you guys and Johnny."

Gino made his way back behind the bar and lined up a dozen shot glasses, then flipped a bottle of whiskey upside down, filling each glass.

"To Johnny!" Little Nick bellowed as he raised the first glass.

"To Johnny!" the rest of the guys said in unison as they raised their own.

The hours wore on with the ever-increasing stack of empty beer bottles and shot glasses filling up the bar counter and tables. Everyone traded stories of Johnny, with a careful eye on Sal, who remained quieter than the rest and drinking less. Little Nick watched Sal walk away alone with his beer in hand, to go sit at a back table.

"So, how're we gonna play this?" Little Nick asked as he

pulled out a chair for himself at Sal's lonely table. Rip was by his side, and Sal looked up from his beer at them.

"Whaddya mean?"

"We gotta get those goddamn bastards back. Hit 'em where it hurts. So what's our plan?"

Sal looked back at his beer and took a sip. He'd heard rumblings of revenge all day long, but the guys were too wary of Sal's mood to bring it up to his face. It seemed like there was a general understanding that he needed the day to mourn — or at least there was an understanding until the drinks started flowing so freely.

"No," Sal said as he gently set the bottle back on the scarred wooden table that he kept his eyes on.

"No?" Nick said. "What do you mean, 'no'?"

"I said, no," Sal said, looking up at both Nick and Rip with the eyes that Rip recognized from the night he showed up at Sal's house. "We're not starting a war."

"But they started it!" Nick said, incredulously.

"Yeah, and you wanna be like them?" Sal suddenly roared as he blasted out of his seat, the wooden chair skidding across the floor behind him. The rest of the bar fell silent. "They're scum. They don't care about lives. They don't care who they hurt. They don't care if there's mothers burying kids. And they damn sure don't care about making people suffer. And suffer over nothin'. Territories? Race sheets? Loan sharking? That's what they're gonna kill somebody over? Somebody who didn't even have a chance to have a family of his own or get out of this goddamn shithole neighborhood? You're not going to be like them," he said, pointing a finger into Nick's chest. As the two made eye contact, Sal backed away.

Sweeping a hand over the room, he finished: "None of you. None of you are gonna be like them! Not if I got anything to say about it."

The entire gang and Gino froze in place, thunderstruck. Only Nick had the nerve to speak.

"So what the hell do you propose we do, Boss?"

"I'll take care of it. This isn't going any further."

No one understood, but no one was going to question Sal anymore. If Little Nick was silenced, the rest of the group sure as hell was too.

————))(())((————

Three days later, Sal walked into Patsy's again with knots in his stomach and dabbed his face with his handkerchief, wiping the heat of the summer away. It was 2 a.m. and the summer heat still hadn't let up. He was sweating more than usual and not just because of the heat, though he would never admit it. In some ways though, this was the biggest day of Sal's life, and his stomach was in knots.

As Sal pulled open the heavy wooden door of the bar, the first face he saw was Gino's. From behind the bar, Gino nodded somberly at Sal. Sal tipped his hat to Gino then set his sights straight ahead, where he saw six faces, most looking agitated.

Inside, Sal smiled to himself. He knew that being fashionably late wouldn't exactly help make him friends, but he damn sure wasn't going to be the one sitting there, wanting to jump out of his skin waiting for crime bosses of the five families to show up. It was his way of getting the upper hand. His turf, his terms, his meeting.

"Gentlemen," he said as he nodded and took off his hat, setting it on a table in the center of the room. Nunzio and Gino had generously donated their bar for the site of Sal's big meeting after hours, so the whole place was his. Sal sat down at the table and gestured for the other men to pull up chairs. "How 'bout this heat huh? You know, before long, we're gonna be back to snow."

"Cut the bull, Sal. We ain't here for a weather report," said one of the men.

"You're here for whatever reason I say you're here," Sal said sternly, that deadly look in his eyes. His guests glanced at each other, gauging reactions.

Sal almost couldn't believe he was in this position. He'd used his family ties to organized crime and had his cousin Al Walker arrange for the boss of the Bonanno family, Giuseppe "Joseph" Bonanno, to gather the heads and underbosses of the other four families — Colombo (Profaci at the time), Gambino, Genovese (Luciano) and Lucchese — to talk to Sal. It was by no means any small accomplishment, and they all required Joe Bonanno's word that Sal wasn't just gathering them up to turn them in to his cop brother. Apparently, they were satisfied enough by Sal sending the reminder that he wasn't exactly keeping his nose clean and had a lot to lose himself by Tony getting involved, because here they all were, bosses and underbosses of the five families: Frank Costello, Giuseppe "Joe" Profaci, Vincent Mangano, Tommy Lucchese, and, of course, Joe Bonanno and Al Walker.

"Look, one of you guys whacked the most kind-hearted

kid I've ever known. And you did it for a bullshit reason," Sal started.

"We don't whack anyone," Tommy said.

"You know goddamn well what I mean," Sal said, staring daggers into the man. "I know you didn't do it yourself — you think I'm stupid?"

The men in the room exchanged glances, and some readjusted in their seats or straightened their neckties, but none spoke.

"I don't know who ordered the hit. I don't wanna know, because if I do find out, I'm gonna take matters into my own hands. But Johnny never did anything to nobody and he didn't deserve to be left floating face down in the goddamn East River," Sal growled, his face getting red. "I'm putting an end to this now, before it gets worse. One of you guys wanted to declare war. Well I'm not biting. We're not doing it."

"So you're waving the white flag?" Mangano asked, a smirk on his face.

"First, you don't wave a white flag when you're not in a war. Second, if you think this is a surrender, you've got another thing coming."

"So what are you saying, Sal?" Frank Costello asked.

"We're moving forward. I'm not getting any blood on my hands and I'm not letting any of my guys — or any innocent person in my neighborhood, for that matter — fall to you wise guys. My guys are hungry for revenge. They want a war. I'm not gonna let this become a war. I just want my territory between the bridges and I don't want to be bothered. This neighborhood is nothing to you guys anyway. Is it really worth people dying for? I don't bother any of you and I want you to respect my territory. Things are tough here and people need help and I'm helping 'em. You guys hide up in your fancy penthouses or Long Island estates and wave your hand to order these hits that don't mean anything to you. Meanwhile, I'm here on the streets with my guys — with my people — and looking out for them. Who are you looking out for besides yourselves?" Sal looked around the room at each man.

"So here's what I want: I want my neighborhood to be my territory and I don't want any trouble. I've got enough bullshit to worry about without wondering if one of your goons is gonna bump off one of my guys, or worse, someone accidentally attached to us. If you agree to back off, when I'm ready to walk away, I walk away and you guys figure out whose territory it becomes."

"And what if we don't agree?" asked Mangano.

Sal let out a small chuckle. "If you don't agree, then you'll get the war you apparently want, and I guarantee you won't win. Because I'm not gonna be hiding away somewhere eating caviar off fine China while I send guys to fight my war. I'll bring the war directly to you — not your soldiers."

For the first time since the meeting began, Joe Bonanno spoke up. "You obviously got my support," he said to Sal. Then, to the rest of the guys, "Look, what do we got to gain by stickin' it to 'em? He's helping people in a little neighborhood that we're all doin' fine without. We ain't losing anything."

"We ain't gainin' either," said Joe Profacci, to grumbles of agreement.

"It just ain't worth it. I say we let him do his thing here

and help people out. We've got other places we can expand to. And we'll get this neighborhood later on, when it makes more sense," Bonanno said. Beside him, Al Walker sat, not saying a word. The room fell silent as the men contemplated their positions, some taking longer than others.

"You got nerve, kid," chimed in Costello, extending his hand to shake Sal's. "I gotta respect that. You've got my word."

And with the heads of two of the five crime families on-board, the others became more persuaded. Nunzio Anastasia was next to agree, encouraged by his friend Frank's gesture of going along with Sal's demands. No one wanted to give up his footing or respect from the other four families, so everyone fell in.

Sal looked around at the powerhouses of men, some of the most respected and feared men in New York. They had all but bowed down to him. The men toasted to their truce with Sal and left the meeting having newfound respect for the twenty-three-year-old.

With bosses of the five major crime families of New York out the door of the bar, Sal took a deep breath and leaned forward, his head in his hands, propped on the table. It made his skin crawl — almost literally, it felt — to be in the same room as those guys. The stuff they had their hands in was too dirty for Sal to comprehend and he wondered how men managed to lose all morals and ethics. He wasn't any saint, he knew that, but there was a line he wasn't willing to cross, and those crime families practically erased any lines that they may have ever had.

RICHARD MANCUSO & JACQUELYN GUTC

The Lake House

Of everything my dad had told me over the last two days, this latest piece of the story was by far the most outrageous and hard to believe. Sure, he'd been surrounded by the major names of Lower East Side fame during his younger days, but this was just shocking. Bosses and underbosses from all five crime families in one room? In Dad's favorite bar? Because of my dad? Sure, I'd always thought he was a genius, but this was almost too much — even for me. To have men, especially these men, give in to a kid half their age blew me away.

But as I was trying to process all of this, a memory from my childhood came rushing into my head.

"You know ... this all seems nuts, Dad," I said. He chuckled.

"Yeah, I can't say you're wrong."

"But I have this memory that's popped into my head off and on throughout my whole life. I never really knew why or what it meant, but I think it makes sense now," I said. I explained to him the vivid memory that I felt like I was able to jump right into.

I was five or six years old and went into the Italian social club that my grandpa had been part of, the Catania club on Henry Street. I loved going in there and getting a soda from this dime machine that would deliver your drink to you via a sort of maze, and you had to grab the bottle just right, or it would get stuck. One day, I ventured into the club for my favorite soda — 7-Up — when this older man who was probably in his sixties said hi. I looked up and saw him lounging at one of the tables in a crisp, beige tailored suit with a white shirt, the look completed with a stick pin that went under his paisley tie and connected each end of the collar.

"Ricardo, avanti, vene qui," he said —"Richard, come here quickly."

"Your father is the toughest man to come outta this neighborhood. Even the made men wouldn't mess with your father," he told me. Though his thick Italian accent made it sound more like, "Yua fadda, isa da tuffist man to come-a outta disa neighborhood, even da made-a men won'ta messa witha yua fadda."

At such a young age, the statement didn't really mean anything to me, but it had floated into my mind over the years. And I remembered how, walking down the street, my father commanded a sort of respect that the average man didn't. Some people would say hi to him as they passed on the street, but even those who didn't would tip their hat to him. I never understood the reasoning for any of this until Dad finally opened the story of his life to me and shared his faceoff of sorts with the crime bosses and made men.

Chapter 17
Finally Ready

With Sal's assurances from the five families that they would stay out of his business, he tried to go on with business as usual. After all, people were still out of work, and they needed him. But there was a heaviness that wasn't there before.

Not wanting to concede anything to the families yet, Sal got Milty Feldman to run the race sheet business citywide, as it had expanded to over two hundred locations. Meanwhile, Ceci took over at the newspaper stand. At this point, Sal's relationship with the brothers who owned the stand had gone on for so many years that they trusted him when he said he had someone to take over selling papers for them in Johnny's place. But it was tough. Ceci hated working the newspaper stand and especially working nights, but he was willing to do it out of loyalty to Sal. Sal agreed to give him a bigger cut in order to keep him happy. Although it made sense to Ceci and the rest of the gang for Sal to hire a kid from the neighborhood who would want to learn the business, Sal silenced this idea. Not only did he not want to trust his original business to a stranger, but he definitely didn't want to get a kid involved in their illegal work.

Plus, the life-altering events of the past year had gotten Sal's mind on the future more than ever — the endgame. He wasn't interested in starting his own crime family, and if he got into the business of recruiting, that probably wouldn't be too far off.

By the following fall, Sal began to see the people in the neighborhood seemingly move on without him. September 1, 1939, brought the official start of the Second World War, as Germany and Russia invaded Poland. Although the United States wasn't officially involved, the wheels of industry began turning again, pulling Americans out of the depths of desperation they had been in for nearly the past decade, and instead giving them a sense of purpose and determination to help defeat the enemy. Guys from between the two bridges went back to work making ammunition in New Jersey or uniforms for the British as companies converted from making consumer products to necessities of war. Increasingly, Sal was forced to weigh the risks of his business against the good it was doing for the people of his community, and he wasn't so sure it was worth it. Fewer people needed his help as a matter of keeping a roof over their heads and food on the table. Now, people wanted bigger loans to start businesses, loans that banks still weren't giving. Sal helped the men get their businesses going, but loaning more money to fewer people had its own downsides. When someone didn't make payments because they'd been overly optimistic about their business, the stakes were higher, and Rip and Little Nick had more of a job to do when they came knocking.

Watching all of the changes around him, Sal decided by 1941 that it was time for him to change his life along with everyone else changing theirs.

Late one morning in June, Sal walked over to the small kitchen table, ready for his meal that was more of a brunch than breakfast each day. He'd had one of his typical late nights with the guys that turned into being out well into the morning hours. Jenny walked over from where she'd been adjusting the radio in the living room and gave him a kiss with a smile.

"Morning," she said as she set a cup of coffee down on the table in front of him, before walking back over to fiddle with the radio.

Sal took a sip of his coffee and swallowed.

"I got a job," he said.

Jenny looked up at him suddenly from where she had been kneeling and abruptly stood up and walked over to the table. "What do you mean? You already have a business that makes us more money than we need. You definitely don't need more jobs."

Sal shook his head and took her hand, leading her to sit at a chair at the table. He stared into her eyes for a moment, seeing that she almost looked scared of what he was saying.

"I'm getting out — going straight. It's time," he said, taking another sip from his coffee while staring at Jenny. She looked shocked at first, but then cleared her face of obvious emotion. She knew he'd been thinking about this for a long time, but was somewhat surprised that it was actually happening. She wasn't sure whether to be happy or sad, excited or nervous.

"So ... what are you going to do? What happens to the business?" she asked him. She didn't ask why. She knew why. Fewer people needed him now, and his mother, brother, Tony, and Tom Dewey had been relentless over the past few years.

"I got a job at the Navy Yard being a laborer. As for the business ... I'm just going to give it to Al Walker and the Bonnano family."

Jenny's eyes widened. "You're going to be a laborer?"

"Yeah, but hopefully not for long. I can work my way up. What else am I gonna do? I don't care what they say — the war is coming. They're hiring like crazy over there. I'd be an idiot to not jump onboard. The money's all right. Other people do it, we can do it. We'll be fine."

"What about the guys?"

"They'll be fine too. No one is having trouble getting work around here these days. They'll probably just have to bust their asses a little more than they're used to," he chuckled a little.

"Well, you know I support whatever you decide, and especially anything that's going to keep you and our family safer."

"This will be good, Jenny. You'll see. We'll just have a normal life, and it'll be good. Now, I just gotta tell the guys."

———

That night, Sal gathered the usual gang at Patsy's. For the first hour, everything went on as normal. He hated to ruin the guys' good time, but he had to tell them the news before too much alcohol was consumed and they panicked or reacted irrationally. He summoned them all to the back of the bar where only the most serious conversations took place. The rest of the guys got serious too, as they followed Sal back there, knowing the fun times usually didn't continue back there.

Sal felt a lump in his throat as he looked out at all of his closest friends and confidants. "Things are changing, guys. We all know it. Guys are back to work and this war is coming. People don't need us like they used to. They're moving on, and it's time we did the same. We had fun. We helped the guys who were down. But we've gotta recognize the writing on the wall and move forward."

"What are you sayin' Sal?" Little Nick asked, afraid of the answer.

Sal took a breath. He knew this was the right thing, but it was still hard to say it to all these guys who had been so loyal. He didn't want to let them down.

"We're closing up shop. Going straight — totally straight."

The guys looked around murmuring incredulously.

"You know I always told you guys to keep your day jobs. The moron gangsters get the attention because they don't have legitimate jobs. Some of you, like Louie, have got jobs and you'll be fine. The rest of you," he said looking at Rip and Little Nick, "you'll be fine. There's more work out there every day. And I'll help you as much as I can if you need it." He thought for a moment, while everyone let the news sink in. "But what I do not want to happen is for any of you — any of you — to keep up with this business we're in now. I'm giving the business to Al Walker and it'll make more money for the Bonannos. You know what we stand for though. I don't want to see any of you get mixed up in their world. You got me? We did enough. We helped people who needed it. We aren't doing things their way. I want each of you to give me your word that you'll wash your hands of all this when we close up."

They all nodded and murmured their agreement.

"And another thing to get straight – this is the end of the business, but not of us. We got each other's backs and this neighborhood is a big part of who we were, and I expect to be sitting in this bar and getting Chinese with you guys every week still. I wouldn't have it any other way."

Sal's own way of showing affection for his friends was enough for them.

"Well," Rip said, raising a glass, "We've been pretty damn good at not worrying about the future and I say we put it off for one more night and have fun before worrying about jobs tomorrow. It's been a hell of a ride, and we have you to thank for all of it, Sal. You got us all through the worst times this neighborhood has ever seen. To Sal!"

"To Sal!" the others mimicked, clinking their glasses together in solidarity, in the shadowy bar, somewhere between the two bridges.

Afterword

The day my dad called me to come see him in New York, I never could have imagined the stories he had to tell. Those days spent at the lake house with him became days I will forever cherish. The whole thing was made even more meaningful because of the fact that I was the only person he trusted his past with. Some of it was so fantastic in an unbelievable way that I was compelled to confirm his stories with as many remaining family members and friends from the old neighborhood as I could. Between the bits and pieces they each remembered, it was clear that the stories my dad shared with me during our days at the lake house weren't a result of his memory playing tricks on him in his old age.

My dad did leave the business, and he gave it to the Bonanno family, by way of his cousin, Al Walker. Throughout my life, there would be times when Dad would say that Walker owed him, and I never knew why, until he shed light on everything at the lake house.

Little Nick, Rip and the other members of my dad's gang were all good guys at heart, and thanks to the gearing up of

World War II, had no trouble finding legitimate work — albeit work that probably wasn't as much fun for them as being my dad's muscle probably was. Rip took a job with the post office while Little Nick went the route that my dad and many other guys from the neighborhood did and worked at the Brooklyn Navy Yard.

When my dad took the job at the Navy Yard in the summer of 1941, he quit his job at the Riis House and he, my mother, and sister, Patricia, moved out of the apartment there. They moved into an apartment on Catherine Street, which would be my home too, right until the week before my eleventh birthday in May, 1956, when we would move to Staten Island.

My dad was tough and could be terrifying in his own quiet way, but he was also an intellectual. When he took the job at the Navy Yard, he wasn't thrilled about being a laborer, and the work was back-breaking. But fortunately, he got the attention of someone higher up. Within months, Horace Weston, a Navy Commander from a well-to-do New England family, called my dad into his office. Weston liked how my dad communicated with the men on the docks and thought he could step in as supervisor where a lot of other, weaker men had failed. Just like that, my dad was second in command at the Navy Yard, overseeing 70,000 men.

When Dad received his draft notice, Weston gave him two options. Whether he decided to get a Navy commission or stay civilian, he would still be second man in command under Weston. Many times over those years, my dad was approached by crime families to look the other way, but when he walked away from the business, he completely walked away, and he refused to get involved with any of the five families. He could hardly believe that they had the gall to want to steal from the government, jeopardizing the lives of our boys.

My dad always said the only things that couldn't be taken away from a man were his name and reputation and he fiercely defended both. He made a decent living and supported his family, and still went out carousing with the guys till all hours of the night, until moving to the suburbs. But as the Depression would forever alter my dad's life, so did the end of the war. At the time Dad turned down the commission, he didn't realize the impact it would have on him in 1946. Staying a civilian had been the wrong decision. He had been told that he was essential during the war, but when the veterans returned, he was easily replaced. My dad lost his job at the docks, and he found himself unemployed with no options. From 1946 to 1949, our family struggled to get by and no one came to our rescue. The Depression took the child out of my dad, but what came after the war hardened him. For our entire lives, my sister and I heard warnings from my dad about preparing for the future. It all made so much more sense to me as I sat listening to his real life story at the lake house that summer in 2001. He and his buddies lived like rockstars, but they only lived for the day, as twenty-somethings tend to do. But his lack of foresight and planning — despite having a family — meant he was left with nothing to fall back on. No nest egg or rainy day money to access when times became desperate. He learned the hard way that, just because you are there for someone, doesn't mean they'll be there for you, and that shaped who he was for the rest of his life.

I remember how a small child in our family once asked my uncle whether my dad ever smiled. My uncle responded, "Sure. Before the Depression." I wonder what it would have been like to know that man, that kid, who laughed and had fun with his friends. Who didn't feel the heavy burden of life's struggles weighing on him every day. Yet, at the same time, I find myself grateful for my dad's experiences, because he was the toughest person I ever knew and absolutely the smartest. We didn't always see eye-to-eye. He didn't talk much and was very no-nonsense, but you always knew where you stood with him, and he was always the kind of guy you'd want on your side.

Somewhere between New York and Colorado at 32,000 feet, it dawned on me that Dad was still Honest Sal, a 1930s Robin Hood and truly The Good Don.

Acknowledgements

We would like to thank our families — in particular, Chris Mancuso, Debbie Pasko and Chris Shepard — for their support from the beginning of this project through publication of the book.

Thank you to our proofreaders and editors who helped get us to the final product with their insight, thoughtfulness and attention to detail: Patricia Mancuso Ravalli, Cyndi Fisher, Bob Guisto, Robert and Lois Van Buskirk, and Bill Luthin.

Special thanks to Franco and the crew at Dolce Sicilia who let us log dozens of hours at their café as we sipped coffee and tea and ate delicious biscotti and other treats while recreating Sal's world. *Grazie mille!*

Sal (right) at his confirmation in 1924 with his godfather, Uncle John Occhipinti.

Card game on Henry Street in 1927.
Sal looks on with his arms around his buddies.

Sal's parents, Peter and Josephine, in their garden on Staten Island around 1933.

Tony Mancuso's wedding in 1934 with Sal as the best man.

Sal showing his boxing talents at Madison Square Garden in February 1934.

Sal at Ravenhall swim club in Coney Island with his oldest brother, Tony, and youngest brother, Phil, around 1934.

Sal and Jenny were married on January 2, 1936.

Sal with his godson, Connie Occhipinti, in fall 1936.

*Sal with Jenny and her cousin, Gloria Scuderi, at the
New York World's Fair in 1939.*

Sal and Jenny at the beach on Coney Island with their two-year-old daughter Patricia.

Sal with Phil Occhipinti, Murphy Mancuso and Jenny in 1940,
getting ready to step out on the town.

World War II begins and a banner near the Riis House displays the patriotism of the neighborhood.

CPSIA information can be obtained
at www.ICGtesting.com
Printed in the USA
FSOW03n1011060217
30464FS